the Lyrics

the Lyrics

compiled by

JANIE L. HENDRIX

Jimi Hendrix: The Lyrics
Compiled by Janie L. Hendrix

All lyrics copyright Experience Hendrix LLC
PO Box 88070
Seattle, WA 98138
www.jimihendrix.com
ISBN: 0-634-04930-5

Published by Hal Leonard Corporation
7777 West Bluemound Road
PO Box 13819
Milwaukee, WI 53213

Trade Book Division Editorial Offices
151 West 46th Street, 8th floor
New York, NY 10036

Visit us online at www.halleonard.com

Library of Congress Cataloging-in-Publication Data
Applied For

Australian Music Trade
Hal Leonard Australia Pty Ltd
22 Taunton Drive
Cheltenham East, VIC 3192
Ph: 61 (0)3 9585 3300
Fax: 61 (0)3 9585 3399
E-mail: aussales@halleonard.com

Australian Book Trade
Gary Allen Pty Ltd
9 Cooper Street
Smithfield, NSW 2164
Ph: 61 (0)2 9725 2933
Fax: 61 (0)2 9609 6155
http://www.garyallen.com.au

Printed through Colorcraft Ltd., Hong Kong
Printed in China.

Exclusive sales and distribution in the UK and EU:
Omnibus Press 8/9 Frith Street London W1D 3JB
http://www.omnibuspress.com

TABLE OF CONTENTS

THE LYRICS

P R E F A C E

Nearly three decades after his untimely death on September 18, 1970, Jimi Hendrix remains an icon of immense power. He is hailed by a succession of generations as an innovative creative force, unrivaled by those who have followed in his outsized footsteps. That he was able to build such an invincible reputation over the course of just four years is nothing short of remarkable. An international following that encompasses nations, languages, races, and genders now dwarfs those who were fortunate enough to actually have felt the searing heat of his creativity in person. The majority of us may have got there too late to appreciate him first hand, but the rich musical legacy he left behind continues to provide a wellspring of inspiration and pleasure.

Hendrix rose to prominence in a decade blissfully free of the entanglements that would have stunted his meteoric ascension had he the misfortune of launching his career today. In 1966, there were no intrusive A&R strategists, no monopolistic corporate control of radio stations, no bowing to win the fleeting fancy of MTV, no tour support to lobby for, no listener flyaways to be bartered for radio airplay, no corporate synergy to foul up Jimi's freak flag flying, free form vision. Jimi took direction from his heart and soul and made it up as he went along, selecting the clothes, hairstyle, and music that uniquely expressed his vision. That is not to say that Hendrix emerged wholly formed within a flowers and sunshine, peace and love, utopian vision of paradise. Nothing could be further from the truth. As a scuffling sideman for R&B stars such as Little Richard, Hendrix had experienced the bitter taste of failure and rejection on more than one occasion. Jimi scrapped and hustled his way to the top from the moment he relocated to London, beginning with his benefactor and co-manager Chas Chandler pawning his last bass guitar to pay for recording time to securing a payola deal to get UK pirate radio airplay for "Hey Joe," to accepting then desperately begging off an opening slot on the Monkees 1967 US tour.

As in everything he did during his dramatic four year career, Jimi Hendrix went about things differently. Unlike other stars of his era, Jimi Hendrix had no Graceland, no castle or sprawling estate to publicly validate his success. Until his death, he lived in a modest, two bedroom apartment in Greenwich Village. Where other contemporaries like the Beatles and Bob Dylan either willingly or unknowingly signed their songs and master tapes over to record companies, Hendrix controlled his creativity and destiny.

Consequently, as his fame and finances rose, Jimi increasingly made the recording studio his creative home, the safe haven where he could write, experiment, or simply jam with friends. The mounting costs troubled his management and legal advisors, but Hendrix was typically unconcerned. "The money doesn't mean anything to me because that's what I make it for, to make better things," he explained in a 1967 interview.

One of Hendrix's dreams was realized in 1970 with the opening of Electric Lady Studios, his state of the art recording facility in the heart of his adopted home, Greenwich Village. The remarkable amount of work he realized there in the few months before his death fueled speculation as to what might have come of future projects with the likes of Stevie Wonder, Miles Davis, George Clinton, and perhaps in later years, Prince and Public Enemy. "Inside the studio we were never bothered by outside influences," remembers Jimi's bassist Billy Cox. "We were left to create music and that's what we loved to do. That made Jimi so happy. He would say, 'Man we don't fish or go bowling like other people do. We make music, and this is fun.'"

What is made unmistakably clear by the remarkable body of music that he managed to compose and record during the last four years of his life is that Jimi Hendrix was teeming with creativity. Music, lyrics, drawings, and poetry seemingly poured out of him during that prolific span. That Hendrix was a supreme instrumentalist and a technical innovator bar none has long been established. *Jimi Hendrix: The Lyrics* presents his considerable gifts as a composer.

This journal illustrates one more compelling aspect of the extraordinarily creative journey Hendrix traveled in those four years. *Jimi Hendrix: The Lyrics* presents his most treasured works in alphabetical order.

Jimi Hendrix: The Lyrics makes no claim to decode Jimi's writings. Fans and friends alike have long tried to decipher Jimi's lyrics, searching unsuccessfully for messages and hidden meanings. Jimi himself provided precious few

...blues, relying instead on creating music that he hoped would transcend superficial pop star adulation and resonate within the hearts and souls of his growing legion of followers. Latter period works such as "House Burning Down," "Power Of Soul," "Machine Gun," and "Earth Blues" made this desire clear.

Presented here in this special collection is a body of compositions which began with "Stone Free", the first song he ever composed for the Jimi Hendrix Experience, and extends through to the material written and considered for *First Rays Of The New Rising Sun*, the ambitious double album sequel to *Electric Ladyland* that he was working on at the time of his death.

Jimi Hendrix, by all accounts, wasn't the type of artist who purposefully set aside time for the specific intent of composing new material. As can be seen by the very papers on which he actually wrote, creating was a full time enterprise for the legendary guitarist. He wrote constantly, brimming with ideas that he felt compelled to document either on tape or on paper. Whether it be the backs of menus, laundry receipts, hotel and airline stationary or just lined yellow or white sheets from pads or notebooks, Jimi was determined to save every phrase and passage that appeared to him. He made countless demos at home and in the studio, massaging these fertile ideas until he was ready to craft a finished master. In the recording studio, one of his cardinal rules for engineers staffing his session was to keep the tapes rolling at all times. In a number of writings featured in *Jimi Hendrix: The Lyrics*, you can see Hendrix make notations as to musical keys, tempos, and other rhythmic ideas he was considering as he committed his thoughts to paper. Perhaps this was so because Jimi was entirely self taught and never learned to read or write music. Such precaution may have been due to Hendrix's desire that none of his ideas be lost or forgotten.

With the passage of time, the study of all things Hendrix continues to intensify. Scholars have been able to pin down what shirt Hendrix wore on a particular night, what his set lists were, and what guitars he preferred to play. What remains elusive however is the source of his measureless creativity, the limitless energy that Hendrix drew on from the very moment former Animals bassist Chas Chandler gave him the gift of opportunity by whisking him to London and pledging to make him a star.

While the root of Hendrix's inspiration may never be fully revealed, what is accepted without dispute is that his songs have stood the test of time. His continuing influence is founded on the compelling appeal and beauty of the songs collected in this book. From the visceral force of "Voodoo Child (Slight Return)" to the majestic beauty of "Little Wing" and "Angel," Jimi's songs continue to inspire artists from around the world to craft their own unique interpretations of his work.

Jimi's songs tended to originate with rhythm patterns he would hone from repeated jamming—although there was no set pattern. Lyrics—especially later in his career as his schedule was increasingly encumbered by a dizzying array of personal appearances—were often completed at the time when Hendrix truly needed them. This process of evolution could be completed in a single session or would be completed just prior to recording his final vocal track in the recording studio. One early draft of "Purple Haze," Jimi revealed in an interview, was at one time more than ten pages long. Other songs like "Room Full Of Mirrors" evolved laboriously over time, shifting in style and tone from blues to rock to funk as Hendrix struggled to capture and define the initial burst of inspiration he had felt .

Jimi never elaborated at great length about his songs. He came to prominence in a vastly different era when self promotion was reserved for the concert stage and an occasional article in *Rolling Stone* or an underground newspaper. Critics outside the counterculture that did take notice of him were initially drawn to his vast skills as a guitarist. Deciphering lyrics was still an exercise reserved for devotees of Lennon & McCartney or Bob Dylan. Some clues as to his methods or lyrical inspiration did however emerge during his live performances. The guitarist often prefaced live renditions of "I Don't Live Today" by dedicating the song to the American Indian. When his themes became more emotional and strident, manifesting themselves, for just one example, as "Machine Gun," Hendrix routinely dedicated the song to people fighting in urban cities such as Milwaukee, Chicago, Birmingham, and Berkeley, and, yes, as he would dryly add, the soldiers in Vietnam. There were indeed, as he remarked famously, so many wars going that he almost forgot.

Jimi Hendrix was successful, handsome, prized his Corvettes, and loved beautiful women. Nearly every one of them remains convinced that he wrote his songs about them. Yet, of all of his female companions, none seemed to inspire more lyrics that Devon Wilson. Jimi's turbulent relationship with Wilson was perhaps best chronicled in "Dolly Dagger." A clear line to Devon can also be drawn within passages in "Freedom," "Crash Landing," and a number of other works.

We do know from Jimi's close friends and associates that certain people and situations found themselves interwoven within his lyrics. Legend has it that the inspiration for "Fire" came from a suggestion made by Noel Redding's mother for Hendrix to warm himself before their fireplace in Kent. According to Faye Pridgon, Sweet Little Annie of "Long Hot Summer Night" was indeed an old Harlem acquaintance. Billy Cox remembers Jimi explaining that "Belly Button Window" was inspired by Mitch Mitchell's pregnant wife Lynn. Jimi felt that Mitch's unborn child was peering out her mother's belly button window taking in all of the sights and sounds of her new world to come. Old Greenwich Village friend Paul Caruso was name checked in "Exp" just as Mama Hanken was prior to the start of Jimi's rendition of "Mannish Boy."

The rest is simple conjecture; did the old Seattle entertainment outpost The Spanish Castle inspire "Spanish Castle Magic" or was it a psychedelic Majorcan vision colorfully captured in a daydream? Who really was that certain "Foxey Lady"? We'll never truly know and perhaps that is what Jimi intended. Jimi Hendrix wanted his music to get inside of those who listened and make people think. Perhaps that remains a fundamental component of its enduring appeal.

John McDermott

Key of D? **1983 - A mermaid I should turn to be**

Jan.-11-14 1968

Horray, I awake from yesterday - alive but the
war is here to stay — So my love (Catherina
and me) - decide to take our last walk through
the noise to the sea
Not to die, but to be reborn - away from
lands, so battered and torn .... forever.

Oh say can you see it's really such a mess
every inch of Earth is a fighting nest — Giant
pencil and lipstick Tube shaped things, continue
to rain and cause screaming pain and the
artic stains from Silver blue to bloody red, as
our feet finds the sand and the sea's just
straight ahead. ———

(Slow march Time) Too Bad, that our friends can't be
with us Today - the machine that we
built would never save us, they say - Impossible
for a man to live and breath under water, forever,
they complained — And any way it would be
beyond the will of God and the grace of the
King. (FADE IN WITH SOLO AND WAR SOUNDS)

A F# A G F# F# E E

Hooray, I awake from yesterday,

Alive but the war is here to stay.

So my love, Catherina, and me

Decide to take our last walk through the noise to the sea.

Not to die, but to be reborn,

Away from lands so battered and torn.

Forever, forever.

Oh say, can you see it's really such a mess,

Every inch of earth is a fighting nest.

Giant pencil 'n' lipstick tube shaped things

Continue to rain and cause screamin' pain.

And the arctic stains from silver blue to bloody red,

As our feet find the sand and the sea, is straight ahead,

Straight up ahead.

Well, it's too bad that our friends,

Ah, can't be with us today.

Well, it's too bad the machine that we built

Would never save us, that's what they say.

That's why they ain't comin' with us today.

And they also said it's impossible

For man to live and breathe underwater,

Forever was a main complaint.

Yeah.

And they also threw this in my face,

They said, uh, anyway, you know good 'n' well

It would be beyond the will of God,

And the grace of the king, grace of the king.

Yeah!

So my darling and I make love in the sand

To salute the last moment ever on dry land.

Our machine has done his work, played his part well,

Without a scratch on our body, and we bid him farewell.

Starfish and giant foams greet us with a smile.

Before our heads go under we take our last look at the killing noise.

Walk the outer style.

The outer style, outer style.

So down and down and down and down and down and down we go.

Hurry my darling we mustn't be late for the show.

Neptune champion games to an aqua world is so very dear.

"Right this way," smiles a mermaid.

I can hear Atlantis full of cheer.

Atlantis full of cheer.

I could hear Atlantis full of cheer.

Lord, thank you.

1983...(A Merman I Should Turn To Be)

A fifty years they've been married
And they can't wait for the fifty first to roll around.
Yeah, roll around.
A thirty years they've been married,
And now they're old and happy and they settle down,
Settle down. Yeah!
Twenty years they've been married,
And they've did everything that could be done.
You know they had their fun.
And then, you came along and talk about…

So you, you say you wanna be married.
I'm gonna change your mind!
Wow! Gotta change.
That was the good side, baby,
Here come the bad side.

Ten years they've been married
A thousand kids running 'round hungry
'Cause their mama's a louse!
Daddy's down at the whiskey house.
That ain't all!

Three years they've been married,
Now they don't get along so good
'Cause they're tired of each other,
You know how that goes.
She's got another lover.
Huh! Same old thing.

So now you're seventeen
Running around, hanging out an' a having your fun.
Life for you has just begun, baby!

And then you come saying;
So you, you say you wanna get married.
Aw, baby, try'n' to put me on a chain.
Ain't that some shame?
You must be losing your, (inhale) mm, sweet little mind!
I ain't ready yet, baby.
I ain't ready.
I'm gonna change your mind.
Look, out baby.

I ain't ready to get tied down.
I ain't ready, I ain't ready now.
Let me live a little while longer.
Let me give, let me live a little while longer.
Look, so if you're finished talkin',
Let me get back in my groove.

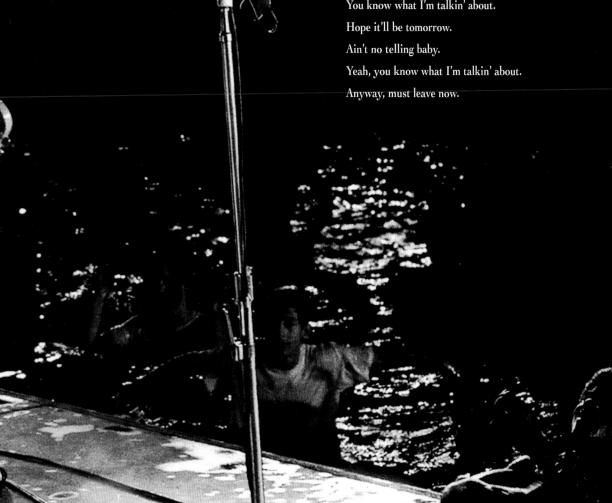

Well, there ain't no,

Ain't no

Ain't no tellin' baby.

When you will see me again,

But I pray it will be tomorrow.

Well, the sunrise

Sunrise

Is burnin' my eyes baby.

Well, now I must leave now,

But I really hope to see you tomorrow.

Well my house is, oh, such a sad mile away.

The feelin' there always hangs up my day.

Oh, Cleopatra, she's driving me insane,

She's trying to put my body in her brain.

So just kiss me goodbye, just to ease the pain.

Sing it, hah!

Ain't no

Ain't no

Ain't no tellin' baby.

Ain't no tellin' babe.

Ain't no tellin' baby when you're gonna see me,

'Cause I really hope it'll be tomorrow.

You know what I'm talkin' about.

Hope it'll be tomorrow.

Ain't no telling baby.

Yeah, you know what I'm talkin' about.

Anyway, must leave now.

Angel

Angel came down from heaven yesterday,

She stayed with me just long enough to rescue me.

And she told me a story yesterday

About the sweet love between the moon and the deep blue sea.

And then she spread her wings high over me.

She said she's going to come back tomorrow.

And I said, fly on my sweet angel,

Fly on through the sky.

Fly on my sweet angel,

Tomorrow I'm gonna be by your side.

Sure enough, this morning came on to me;

Silver winged silhouette against a child's sunrise.

And my angel, she said unto me,

"Today is the day for you to rise.

Take my hand, you're gonna be my man.

You're gonna rise."

And then she took me high over yonder, Lord.

And I said, fly on my sweet angel,

Fly on through the sky.

Fly on my sweet angel,

Forever I will be by your side.

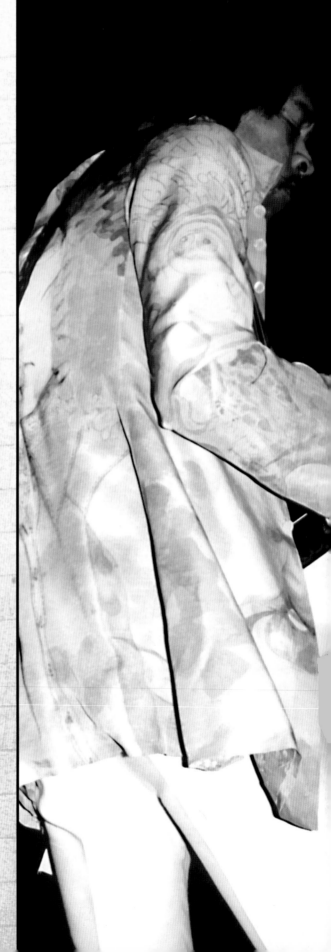

Key of D F# **My Angel** Caterina

(Return of little wing) Finished

Jan. 14 1968

Angel come down from heaven yesterday
She stay just long enough for afternoon tea
And she tell me a story yesterday
about the love between the moon and the deep
blue sea — And when it was time to
go, she spread her wings high over me
and she said , I shall return tomorrow
And I said fly on my sweet angel
          fly on through the sky
     fly on my sweet angel — tomorrow
I will look for you by my side.

And sure enough, this morning comes to me
with silver wings silloette against the glow
of the child sunrise —
And as all the blue birds and the sparrows
envy me — She said I love you little boy
~~and I'm gone~~ ~~Please come fly with me~~ and I ~~can fix~~ will
you how to fly — She ~~touches~~ kiss me once and I
and pure joy made me cry now we can fly together
by wing I said " Now I shall forever be by your side

Beverly Rodeo Hyatt House
360 North Rodeo Drive
Beverly Hills, California

Angel come down from Heaven
yesterday --- She stayed with
me just long enough for to rescue me.
And She tells me a story yesterday -
About the ~~love~~ Love between the moon
and the deep blue sea —
And then She spread her wings
High over me — And She said
`I shall ~~collect~~ Read you ~~tomorrow~~ tomorrow`
And I said "fly on my sweet Angel.
fly on through the sky. fly on my
Sweet Angel; tomorrow I hope to be by
your side —

And Sure enough this
morning comes to me — with Silver
wings sillouette against the glow of
the child son rise —
And my angel She said unto me
"You're ~~have been~~ liveing through me ..
~~But let the~~ still tears in your eyes —
But why are there

forget about living in the past
My Love and try to realize
I have come, to melt away,
Your pain and sorrow ··· forever ··"
And I said "fly on my Sweet angel, fly on through
the Sky .. fly on my Sweet angel — ~~for~~ Help me
through the Sky ·Help me come ~~back~~ take me in your life
alive

Are You Experienced?

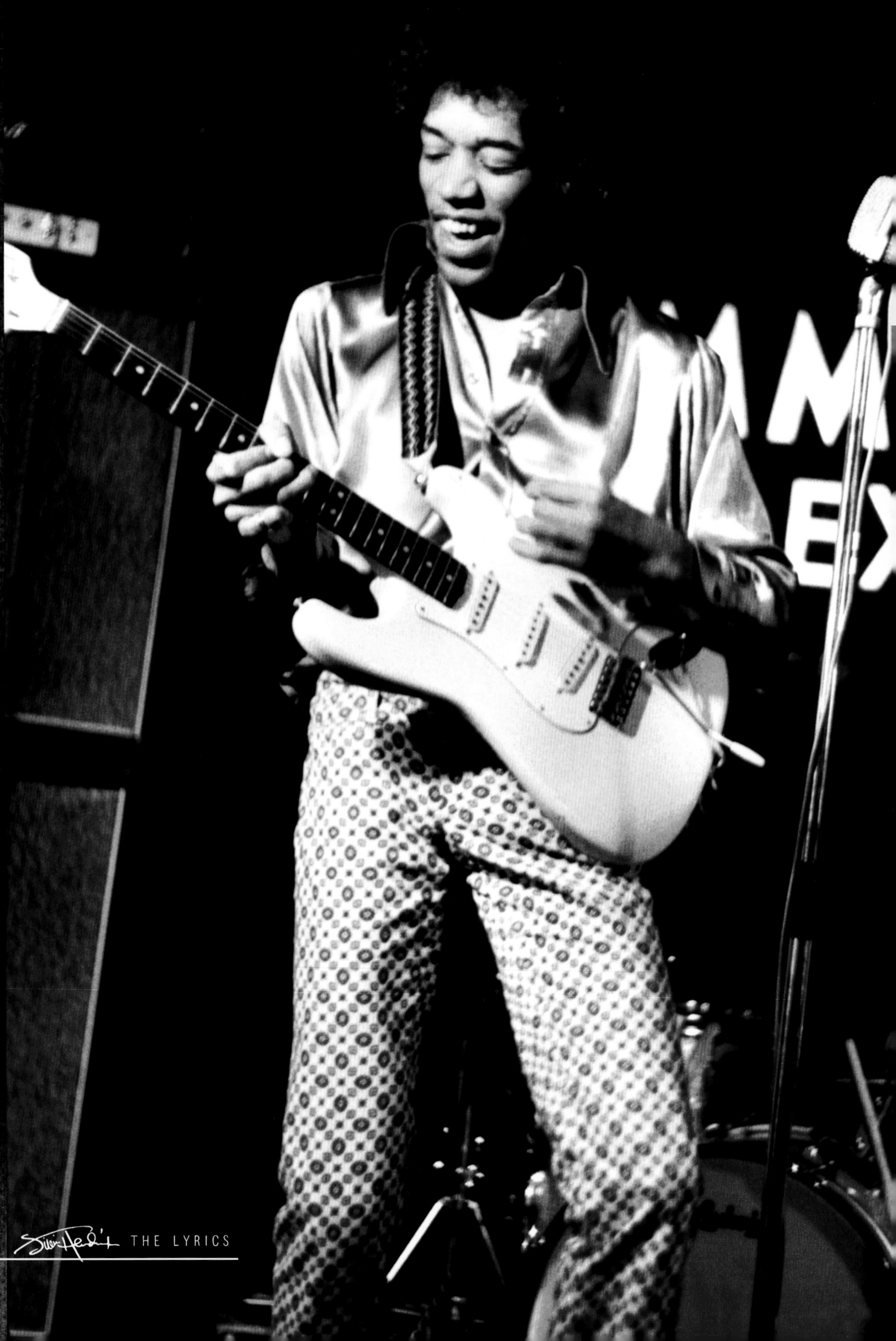

If you can just get your mind together,
Then come across to me.
We'll hold hands and then we'll watch the sunrise,
From the bottom of the sea.

But first, are you experienced?
Have you ever been experienced?
Well, I have.

I know, I know you'll probably scream and cry
That your little world won't let you go.
But who in your measly little world are you trying to prove that
You're made of gold and can't be sold?

So, are you experienced?
Have you ever been experienced?
Well, I have.

Oh, let me prove it to you. Yeah!

Trumpets and violins, I can hear in the distance,
I think they're calling our name.
Maybe now you can't hear them, but you will
If you just take hold of my hand.

Oh, but are you experienced?
Have you ever been experienced?
Not necessarily stoned, but beautiful.

ASTRO MAN and STRATO-WOMAN
THE COSMIC LOVERS
OF THE UNIVERSE and everything

.BASS
like
IZABELLA
No.1.
ROY TAN

please understand what
I'm trying to say

I love the comics so It's easy
to say —··
[READ]

I had a dream just the
other day

that I was... ASTRO-Man

I'm Astro-man .... I'm flying higher than
that faggot Superman ...
ever could ——— ever would.

they call me ASTRO man ...
If you signal, I'll give you a hand..
to Blow out what I can ....
··· in the Rest of your Mind.

(then thrilling suspense type music comes in
?5 narrator gives set-up of
scene

Here I come to save the day.

A little boy inside a dream just the other day,

His mind fell out of a space and the wind blew it away.

A hand came out from heaven and pinned a badge on his chest.

It said "Get out there man and do your best."

And they call him Astro Man,

And he's flyin' higher than

That old faggot Superman ever could.

Ow! They call him cosmic nut,

And he's twice as dense as Donald Duck.

And he'll try his best to screw you up,

The rest of your mind.

Look out now, here it comes.

Astro Man, flyin' across the sky

Two times higher than that old faggot Superman

Ever, ever could, ever could.

There it goes, there it goes.

Where it stops, no one knows.

There it goes, there it goes, Lord.

He's try'n' try'n' to blow up the rest of your mind.

He's gonna blow up the rest of your mind.

Talkin' about livin' for peace of mind.

Astro Man will leave you your pieces.

Have you poop out your behind, baby.

Leave you flyin' around in pieces.

Yeah, talkin' 'bout the rest of your mind.

Astro Man is talkin' 'bout the rest of your mind.

He's gonna blow out the rest of your mind.

Woo hooo

Ya ya ya ya ya yaaaa

Blow out the rest of your mind.

I've been Jesus Christ
—— so twice ...

Super man —— C'mon, throw
the Dice —

Capt. Midnite —— How do I look..

King Out of sight —write a
new Book ——

Whatelse do you have to offer
what else is up for sale

What else do you want to
turn me to ——

this time if it's not me, myself
and I,   all ya'll   May as well go to Hell.

Mr. and Miss Carraige

TELEPHONE 377-5911 Area Code 704
TWX: 704-525-2420

Red Carpet Inn
615 E. MOREHEAD ST. / CHARLOTTE, N. C. 28202

Blue beat
on chorus
verse will be sung
with parade.
beat

1. Well I'm up here in this
womb, lookeing all around --- I look out my
belly button window. and I see nothing but
frowns *   And I think they --- dont want me... around

2. Well what's all this fuss, what seems to be the sham
I mean damn, if they dont want me, hell I'll go back
to spirit land... And even take me a longer rest
before comeing down this chute again ··· Man I remember
the last time ··· they was still argueing about me then-
* And if you dont···· want me now···
please make up your mind··· where and when,

Break → Because I AINT comeing THIS WAY TOO MUCH
MUCH MORE AGAIN   OH NO

3. What is that, is that a doctor, Hey bro' watch
out for that thing — You act like my Potential mixed up
Mama is   carrying an orangutang —
You say how do I know what a monkey is ··· Man
we all been here before··· so as soon as you
People stop pokeing me ··· I'll abliged if you close
that door ···* And make up your mind···· give or take···
you only got···200 days ··· AND THEN (over)

Well, I'm up here in this womb,

I'm lookin' all around.

Well, I'm looking out my belly button window

An' I see a whole lotta frowns.

An' I'm wondering if they don't want me around.

Well, what seems to be the fuss out there?

Just what seems to be the hang?

'Cause you know they just don't want me this time around,

Yeah, I'll be glad to go back to the spirit land,

And even take a longer rest

Before coming down the chute again.

Man, I sho' remember the last time, baby.

They were still arguin' about me then.

So if you don't want me now,

Make up your mind, where or when.

If ya don't want me now, give or take

You only got two hundred days.

'Cause I ain't comin' down this way too much more again.

You know, they got pills for ills 'n' thrills 'n' even spills,

But I think you're just a little too late.

So I'm comin' down into this world, Daddy,

Regardless of love and hate.

I'm gonna sit up in your bed, mama,

and just a, grin right in yo' face.

And then I'm gonna eat up all your chocolates,

Say, "I hope I'm not too late."

So if there's any questions make up your mind,

'Cause you better give or take.

The question's in your mind, give or take.

You only got two hundred days.

Play the blues, man, lookin' all around.

Sure is dark in here.

I'm lookin' out my belly button window,

An' I swear I ain't seen nothin' but a whole lotta frowns.

An' I'm wonderin' if they want me around.

Belly Button Window

Well I'm up here in this
womb --- Lookeing all
around ---
I look out ~~th~~ my belly
button windew, and I see
a whole lot of frowns
And I'm wondering ... if they
want me ... around --

2. well what's all the fuss
out there ... what seems to be
the Shame ---
Cause if they don't want me
around -- Hell, I'll go back to
Spirit Land ---

And even take a longer rest
before comeing down this
Chute again --
Man I remember the last
time ... they were argueing
about me then .
So if you don't ... want me now
make up your mind ... give or take
where and when --- you only get .. 300 days
Cause I aint comeing this way
too much more again .

They got pills, for ills, and
$thrills and even spills
~~regardless of love or hate~~.
But I think you're just alittle
too late .
So I'm comeing on down to this
world Daddy ... regardless
of love and hate .
... I'm gonna sit up in your
Bed mama and givin in your
face - and then 'I'm gonna
eat up all your chocolates and
Say "I hope I'm not late ." ---

                    you know, people
well ~~you all~~ apt all these pills for chills, ill
and thrills and then when it comes to
s babies, you don't know what you fee
real.. So if you want abortion, by all m
ase go head ~~just use cover~~ Because you know
~~You wont mess me up with safe~~ to bring me up with ~~bo bre~~
          it aint kool

especially when that world outside is
   so cold ~~and dead~~ Hateful and dead
      so legalize, if you're wise
       for me to lay back
              or for
              to rise
      Or else, find something else
  for you all to do

6662

TWA IN FLIGHT

BBW

Mister and Miss Carriage esq.

Well I'm way up in this womb.
lockeing all around—
And when I look through my window
I see nothing but frowns
[I don't know if they really want me
around].

Well I'm due to meet ~~greet~~ them face to face
in about 300 days.
But at night I hear them saying
my arrival may be a disgrace.
(I don't know if they can afford]
(me ~~be~~ comeing around.

next page

USA EUROPE AFRICA ASIA

I don't feel bad on their
attitude about not wanting me
just yet - I'm willing till the
next time to wait in my cozy set
[They say they love me, And it will
better on the next time around -

Well if they want to get rid of me
They better get it together soon
~~But I wish they'd make up their~~
~~mind~~ And maybe the next time, in
my mouth Oh Dad ~~just~~ might ~~show~~
lay a silver spoon - Isn't it a
shame how the lack of ~~money~~ ~~can~~ can rule a life
~~that two young kids~~

Bold As Love

Anger, he smiles, towering in
Shiny metallic purple armour.
Queen Jealousy, envy waits behind him,
Her firey green gown sneers at the grassy ground.
Blue are the life giving waters taking for granted,
They quietly understand.
Once happy turquoise armies lay opposite, ready,
But wonder why the fight is on.

But they're all bold as love.
Yeah, they're all bold as love, yeah!
They're all bold as love.
Just ask the Axis.

My Red is so confident, he flashes trophies of war
And ribbons of euphoria.
Orange is young, full of daring, but
Very unsteady for the first go around.
My Yellow in this case is not so mellow.
In fact, I'm try'n' to say it's frightened like me.
And all these emotions of mine keeps holding me from
Giving my life to a rainbow like you.

But I'm a, yeah, I'm bold as love
Well, I'm bold, bold as love,
Hear me talkin' girl.
I'm bold as love,
Just ask the Axis.
He knows everything...

Yeah, Yeah, Yeah

Jimi Hendrix THE LYRICS

The SHOREHAM
Hotel and Motor Inn
CONNECTICUT AVENUE AT CALVERT STREET
Washington 8, D. C.

Anger smiles, standing in Shiny metallic
Purple armour – Queen Jealousy +
Envy waits behind him – Her fire
green gown laughs at the grassy ground
Blue are the ~~life givving~~ ~~knowing~~ waters, ~~the~~
~~close to them~~ ~~they under stand~~
   takeing for Granted's ~~mother~~ they Quitley
under stand – once happy Torqoise Armys
lays opposite ready, But wondering
   why the fight is on

Yellow in this case) is not so mellow
~~in fact~~, I'm Trying to say, it's
Frightened like me.
But ~~ALL OF THESE~~ is still ~~but rather~~
~~Love it a rainbow~~

And all of these emotions of ~~the~~ mine
keeps holding me from ~~tooking~~ back
~~puting my life~~
~~love to you~~   Giveing my life to
~~my life to you~~   You
   Rainbow

Anger [he] Smiles, ~~stood~~ Towering, in shiny
Mettalic purple armoor - Queen Jealousy
Envy waits, behind him - her fire g'reen
gozun ~~teail~~ sners at the grassy g'round

Blue are the life-giveing waters
Takeing for granted, they Quietly understand.
[once-happy] Torqouise Armys lay oppisite ready
But wondering why the fight is on
But their all bold as love .... Just ask the AXIS.

Red .. [Symbal s] [clash], So confident he ~~curls~~ . flashes
~~words f~~ Trophies of war and
Ribbons of ~~[scribble]~~ ~~pleasure~~ euphoria

Orange is Young, full of daireing
~~to~~ But very ~~[scribbled] at first.~~
UN~~SURE~~ [steady] for the first
so round

YELLOW, ~~IN this case~~) [il. this case] not so Mellow,
IN FACT I'm Trying to say ~~those~~ its
~~[scribble]~~ frightened like me - ~~[scribble]~~ ~~cant~~
~~YOU understand~~ BUT ~~IN the~~ ~~conversation~~
~~YOUR IMAGE~~

The morning is dead
And the day is too.
The step is up here to meet me,
But the velvet fool.
All my loneliness
I have felt today.
It's a little
More than enough to make a man
Throw himself away.
I continue
To burn the midnight lamp alone.

Now, the smiling portrait of you
Is still hanging on my frowning wall.
It really doesn't, really doesn't bother me
Too much at all.

It's just the ever falling dust
That makes it so hard for me to see
That forgotten earring laying the floor,
Facing coolly toward the door.
And I continue
To burn the midnight lamp, all alone.
Burn.

Yeah, yeah.
Lonely, lonely, lonely.
Loneliness is such a drag.

So here I sit today
That same old fireplace
Getting ready for the same old explosion
Goin' through my mind.
And soon enough time will tell
About the surface in the wishing well.
And someone who will by and sell for me
Someone who will tow my bale.
And I continue
To burn the same old lamp, alone.
Yeah! Midnight lamp.
Can you hear me calling you?
So lonely, gotta blow my mind.
Yeah! Yeah!
Lonely, lonely
Midnight Lamp

Burning Of The Midnight Lamp

Can You See Me?

Can you see me
Begging you on my knee?
Oh yeah
Can you see me, baby,
Begging please don't leave?
Alright?
If you can see me doing that, you can
See in the future of a thousand years.

Can you hear me, yeah,
Crying all over town?
Yeah baby
Can you hear me, baby,
Crying 'cause you put me down?
Let's reach up, girl.
If you can hear me doing that, you can
Hear a freight train coming from a thousand miles.

Oh yeah baby

Can you hear me
Singing this song to you?
You better open your ears!
Can you hear me, baby,
Singing this song to you?
Ah, shucks!
If you can hear me sing
You better come home like you s'posed to do.

Can you see me?
Hey hey
I don't believe you can see me.
Oh yeah
Can you hear me, baby?
I don't believe you can.
You can't see me

Jimi Hendrix THE LYRICS

38 *Jimi Hendrix* THE LYRICS

Down the street you can hear her scream, "You're a disgrace,"

As she slams the door in his drunken face.

And now he stands outside

And all the neighbors start to gossip and drool.

He cries, "Oh girl, you must be mad.

What happened to the sweet love you and me had?"

Against the door he leans and starts a scene,

And his tears fall and burn the garden green.

And so castles made of sand

Fall into the sea, eventually.

A little Indian brave, who before he was ten,

Played war games in the woods with all his Indian friends.

And he built a dream that when he grew up

He would be a fearless warrior Indian Chief.

Many moons passed and more the dream grew strong

Until tomorrow he would sing his first war song,

And fight his first battle, but something went wrong.

Surprise attack killed him in his sleep that night.

And so castles made of sand

Melts into the sea, eventually.

There was a young girl whose heart was a frown

'Cause she was crippled for life and she couldn't speak a sound.

And she wished and prayed she could stop livin',

So she decided to die.

She drew her wheelchair to the edge of the shore,

And to her legs she smiles, "You won't hurt me no more."

But then a sight she'd never seen made her jump and say,

"Look, a golden winged ship is passing my way."

And it really didn't have to stop, it just kept on going.

And so castles made of sand

Slips into the sea, eventually.

Come on down hard on me baby
Come on down hard as you can
Come on down hard on me baby
Lord, come on down hard as you can
Come on down hard on me baby
Show me that I'm your lover man.

Come on down hard juicy
Command me as your teddy bear
Bring that love down hard on me baby
Rock me rock me right through the bed.
Come on down hard on me baby,
please show me I'm your lover man

I want to you love you so much I hope we can make it
I want to love you so much I hope I don't break it
I want to love you so much 'til I can't stand it
I want to love you so strong 'til you've got to say you've had it.

Yeah

Crash Landing

Hey! You don't love me girl, but you just want me
So let's make it baby, so I can leave
You don't need me, you just wanna believe
So take out your dagger and cut me free, cut me free, cut me free

Hey! you don't love me girl, you just try to suffocate me ...
So hand me your blankets and take your dirty sheets
Take your dirty, dirty sheets. Take your dirty, dirty...

Well, I must admit that you can be a pretty good artist
But I've never seen that smile painted all across your face

I do declare you should be a rocket.
Well, take a look at how easy you get me spaced out, laid out
Look at the sun fade out.
And you almost made me leave my faith outside.

Yeah, yeah, yeah, yeah, yeah
You don't love me

Hey look at ya, all lovey-dovey when you, mess around with that needle
But, I'm working, how hard would your love be otherwise
I wonder just how would you love me baby
Well dig this

Well, I'm gonna spank your hands and I'm gonna throw away your stupid needle
I'm gonna try to make love straight for the very first and last time
And I'll take it easy this time sugar, unless you want to hurry up and die

You don't love me girl, you just wanna hurt me
So lets hurry and get this scene over so you can marry up with that old sweet
You don't need me, you just wanna see me watch you run after that old silly slimeball
Bounce across the freeway

THE LYRICS

Bang, bang, shoot, shoot

As long as you're yourself girl, I'll try not to give a hoot

Bang, bang

Bang, bang, gun, shoot, shoot, shoot

As long as you're your silly here, I don't give a hoot

Yeah, Slow down, slow down

Bang, bang, shoot, shoot

As long as you're gonna be all messed up, I don't give a damn

Slow down, slow down, slow down

Bang, bang, shoot, shoot,

As long as you're your silly self, I don't give a hoot.

Hey!

You jump in front of my car when you,

You know all the time that,

Ninety miles an hour girl, is the speed I drive.

You tell me it's alright,

You don't mind a little pain.

You say you just want me to take you for a drive.

You're just like crosstown traffic.

So hard to get through to you.

I don't need to run over you.

All you do is slow me down,

And I'm tryin' to get on the other side of town.

I'm not the only soul who's accused of hit and run.

Tire tracks all across your back;

I can see you had your fun.

But darlin' can't you see my signals

Turn from green to red?

And with you I can see a traffic jam straight up ahead.

You're just like crosstown traffic.

So hard to get through to you.

I don't need to run over you.

All you do is slow me down,

An' I got better things on the other side of town.

Look out, baby, comin' through.

Look out, Look out.

What's that in the street?

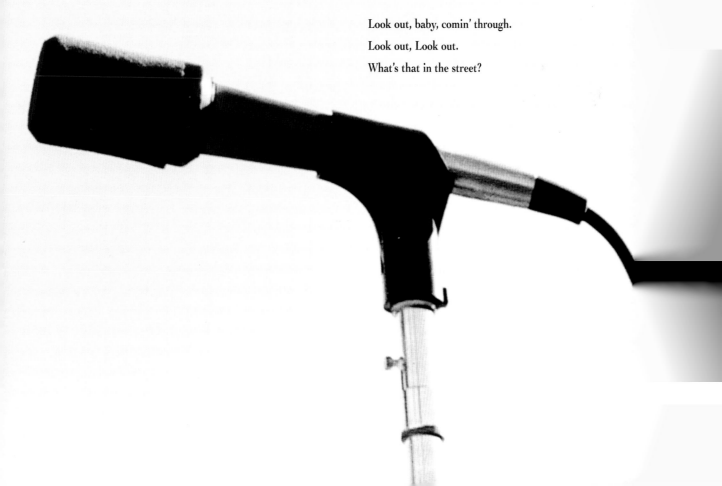

You jump in front of my
(car when you know all)
the time that 90 miles
anhour is the speed I drive

You tell me it's alright, you
~~you don't mind a little pain~~
~~just scratch on ride~~, But By
the ~~&~~ tire tracks ~~on the~~ across
your back, how do you manage)
to stay alive →

Cross town traffic - so hard to get
      through to you
Cross town Traffic - I don't want run
over you.
Cross town traffic - All you do is slow
me down - and I'm tryin' to get to
the other side of town

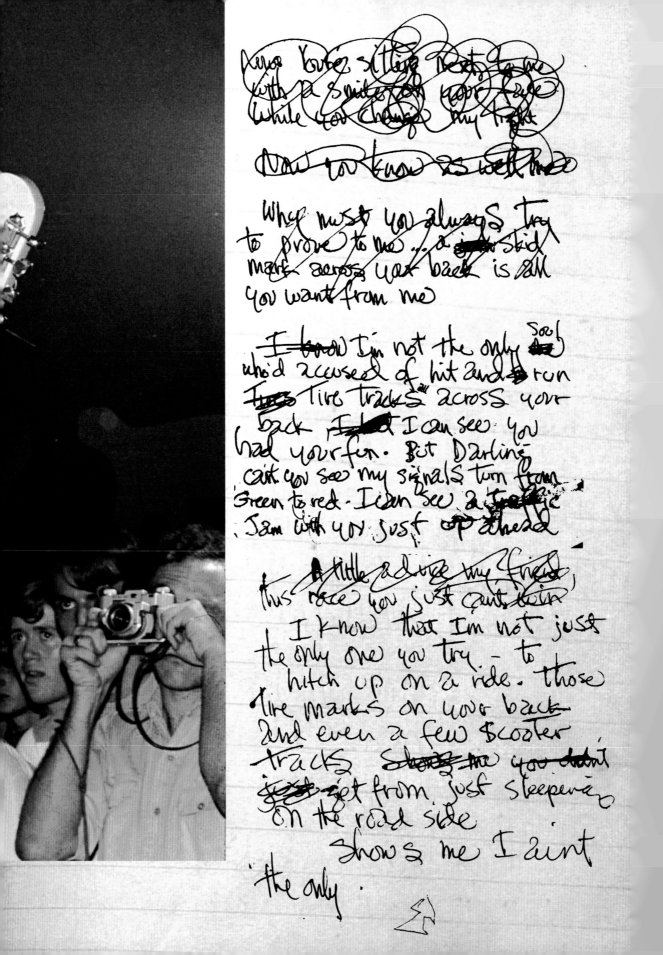

~~You're sitting next to me~~
~~with a smile on your face~~
~~while you change my first~~

~~Now you know as well me~~

Why must you always try
to prove to me ... ~~a~~ ~~skid~~
~~mark across your back~~ is all
you want from me

~~I know~~ I'm not the only soul
who'd accused of hit and ~~run~~
~~Tires~~ Tire tracks across your
back ~~I~~ I can see you
had your fun. But Darling
can't you see my signals turn ~~from~~
green to red. I can see a ~~traffic~~
jam with you just ~~up~~ ahead

~~A little advice my friend,~~
~~this race you just can't win~~
I know that I'm not just
the only one you try - to
hitch up on a ride. those
tire marks on your back
and even a few scooter
tracks ~~shows me you didn't~~
~~just get~~ get from just sleeping
on the road side
            Shows me I aint
the only.

Dolly Dagger

Here comes Dolly Dagger.

Her loves so heavy, gonna make you stagger.

Dolly Dagger, she drinks the blood from a jagged edge.

Aw, drink up, baby.

Been ridin' broomsticks since she was fifteen,

Blowin' out all the other witches on the scene.

She got a bullwhip as long as your life.

Her tongue can even scratch the soul out of the devil's wife.

Well, I seen her in action at the Player's Choice,

Turn all the love men into doughnut boys.

Hey, red hot mama you better step aside,

This chick's gonna turn you to a block of ice.

Look out!

Here comes Dolly Dagger.

Her love's so strong, gonna make you stagger, baby.

Dolly Dagger, she drinks blood from a jagged edge.

Drink up, baby, yeah!

Yeah, look at old burnt out Superman tryin' to shoot his

dust on the sun.

Captain Karma kids, they're dead on the run.

Oh the words of love, do they ever touch Dolly Brown?

Better get some highway and clear outta town.

Here comes Dolly Dagger.

Her loves so heavy, gonna make you stagger.

Dolly Dagger, she ain't satisfied 'til she gets what she's after.

She drinks the blood from the jagged edge.

You better watch out baby, here comes your master.

Alright.

Watch out Devon.

Give me a little bit of that thing.

Dolly, heavy mama, get it on, get it on, get it on.

Dolly, heavy mama, get it on, get it on, get it on.

Dolly, heavy mama, get it on, get it on, get it on.

Dolly, heavy mama, get it on, get it on, get it on, get it on,

get it on, get it on, get it on.

Ohh ohhh Ohhhhhh yeah yeah yeahhh

Ohh ohhh Ohhhhhh yeah yeah yeahhh

Ohh ohhh Ohhhhhh yeah yeah yeahhh

Ohh ohhh Ohhhhhh yeah yeah yeahhh

Ohh ohhh Ohhhhhh yeah yeah yeahhh

THE LYRICS

Drifting on a sea of forgotten teardrops
On a lifeboat sailing for your love, sailing home.

Drifting on a sea of old heartbreaks,
On a lifeboat sailing for your love, sailing home.
Sailing home, sailing.

Jimi Hendrix THE LYRICS

Drifting

Well, I see hands and tearstained faces
Reachin' up, but not quite touchin' the promise land.
Well, I taste tears and a whole lot of precious years wasted
Sayin' to luck please give us a helpin' hand.

Lord, there's got to be some changes.
Gonna be a whole lotta rearranges.
You better hope love is the answer.
Yeah, better come before the summer.

Well, everybody can hear the sound of freedom's bleedin' heart.
Sirens clashin' with earth and rock and stone.
You better love me, but it's gonna be the last time.
And tell the child who buried daddy's old clothes.

Yeah, they're talkin' about getting together, yeah.
Together for love, love, love.
You better hope love is the answer, baby.
I think you better hope it comes before this summer.

Everybody, every sister, every lover,
To feel the light, that's shinin' bright, baby
Everybody, we got to live together.

Right on, baby.
Feel those earth blues comin' at ya, baby!

Don't let your imagination take you by surprise.
I'm cleanin' every eye, one day visualize.
My head in the clouds, my feet all over the place, baby.
Don't get too stoned, please remember you're a man.

Lord, there's got to be some changes.
Livin' together's gonna be a lot of rearranges.
You better be ready, Lord, Lord knows.
Let's hope love comes before the summer.

Everybody, ya got to feel the light,
You got to feel the light, baby.
Everybody, got to live together.
Deep in it together.
Right on together.

Whoah!

All stand together for the earth blues comin' at ya, baby.

Love, love, love.
Right on time.
Right on, baby, right on.
Yeah, let's do it for it's comin' at ya.
Gotta get right on together.
Together.

Ezy Rider

THE LYRICS

There goes Ezy, Ezy Ryder,
Riding down the highway of desire.
He said the free wind takes him higher,
Tryin' to find his heaven above,
But he's dying to be loved.
Dying to be loved.

He's telling me livin' so magic.
He says today is forever, so he claims.
He's talkin' about dying, he's so tragic, baby.
But don't you worry about it today,
We got freedom comin' our way.
Freedom comin' our way, yeah.

How long do you think he's gonna last?
Carry that old gas!
See all the lovers say, "Do what you please."
Gotta get them brothers together and the right to be free.
In a cloud of angel dust, I think I see me a freak!
Hey, motorcycle mama, you gonna carry me?
An' I'll be stone crazy.
Love comin' in kinda hazy.
Stone crazy, baby.

Wowwww!

There goes Ezy, Ezy Ryder,
Riding down the highway of desire.
He said the free wind takes him higher,
Searchin' for his heaven above,
But he's dying to be loved.
Dying to be loved!
Here comes Ezy, Ezy Ryder, baby.
Tryin' to fly higher.
I said Ezy Ryder, baby!
Tryin' to fly higher!
Ezy Ryder! Ezy Ryder!

Fire

Alright! Now dig this baby!

You don't care for me, I don't care about that.
You got a new fool, I like it like that.
I have only one burning desire
Let me stand next to your fire!

Let me stand next to your fire!
Whoa let me stand, baby!
Let me stand. Yeah, baby!
Listen here, baby, and stop acting so crazy.

You say your mom ain't home, it ain't my concern.
Just a play with me, and you won't get burned.
I have only one itching desire,
Let me stand next to your fire!

Let me stand, baby!
Let me stand!
Oh, let me stand!

Ow!

Move over, Rover, and let Jimi take over!
Yeah, you know what I'm talking 'bout!
Yeah! Get on with it baby!

Ow!
Yeah!

That's what I'm talking 'bout.
Now dig this!
Ha!
Now listen baby!

You try to gimme your money, you better save it babe
Save it for your rainy day.
I have only one burning desire,
Let me stand next to your fire!

Let me stand!
Ow!
Oh, let me stand baby!
I ain't gonna do you no harm.

Ow!
Yeah!

You better move over, baby!
I ain't gonna hurt ya, baby!
I ain't talkin' with your ol' lady.
Yes this is Jimi talkin' to you!
Yeah, baby!

Jimi Hendrix THE LYRICS

Foxey!

Foxey!

You know you are a cute little heart breaker.

Foxey!

Yeah!

And you know you are a sweet little lover maker.

Foxey!

I wanna take you home.

I won't do you no harm. No.

You've got to be all mine, all mine.

Ooh! Foxey lady!

Yeah

Foxey!

Foxey!

Now I see, on down on the scene. Oh, Foxey.

You make me wanna get up and scream! Foxey!

Oh, baby listen now.

I've made up my mind.

I'm tired of wasting all my precious time.

You've got to be all mine, all mine.

Foxey lady!

Here I come

Yeah!

I'm gonna take you home.

I won't do you no harm. No.

You've got to be all mine, all mine.

Foxey lady!

Here I come baby, I'm comin' to get ya!

Ow!

Foxey Lady

You look so good

Foxey lady

Oh yeah Wo!

Foxey Lady

Yeah, give us some

Foxey lady

You make me feel like, feel like saying, Foxey

Oh baby

Foxey

Foxey Lady

Foxey Lady

Freedom

You got my pride hangin' outta my bed.

You messing with my life, so I bought my lead.

Even messing with my children, and you screamin' at my wife, baby.

Get off my back, if you wanna get outta here alive!

Freedom! That's what I want now!

Freedom! That's what I need now!

Freedom to live!

Freedom so I can give!

You got my heart, speak electric water.

You got my soul, screamin' and hollerin'.

You know, you hooked my girlfriend, you know the drugstore man.

Well, I don't need it now, I'm just tryin' to slap it out of her hand!

Freedom! So I can live!

Freedom! So I can give!

Freedom! Yeah!

Freedom! That's what I need!

You don't have to say that you love me if you don't mean it.

You better believe.

If you need me, or you just want to bleed me,

You better stick in your dagger in someone else so I can leave.

Set me free!

Yeah!

Keep on pushin', right on, straight ahead!

Stay up an' straight ahead.

Freedom so I can live baby.

Freedom do I chew it up and give, baby!

Freedom so I can be, babe.

Freedom!

Keep on pushin', straight ahead!

Jimi Hendrix THE LYRICS

Gypsy Eyes

well I realize that I've been Hypnotized I love you Gypsy eyes

Up in my tree I'm sitting by my fire,
wondering where in this world tonight
you be. O And knowing all the time,
Your still roaming the country side...
You know that I love y Do you still think about me
Ohmy Gypsy eyes

Well I walk right on up to your rebel
roadside... the one that rambles on
for a million miles. Yes I walk down this
road Searching for my your love and
my soul And... O when I find you, I
aint gonna let go of my Gypsy eyes.

BRIDGE. I remember the first time that I saw you.
The tears in your eyes, they looked alike, they
were trying to say – Oh little Boy you know
I could love you – But first I must make
my getaway – Two strange men fightin to the
death over me today – I'll try to meet you
on the old Highway

Well, I realize that I've been hypnotized.

I love you Gypsy Eyes.

I love you Gypsy Eyes.

Gypsy, way up in my tree I'm sitting by my fire,

Wond'rin' where in this world might you be.

And knowin' all the time you're still roamin' the countryside.

Do you still think about me?

Oh, my. Gypsy.

Well, I walk right on up to your rebel roadside,

The one that rambles on for a million miles.

Yes, I walk down this road searchin' for your love an' my soul too.

When I find ya, I ain't gonna let go.

I remember the first time I saw you.

The tears in your eyes look like they're tryin' to say,

"Oh little boy, you know I could love you,

But first I must make my getaway.

Two strange men fightin' to the death over me today.

I'll try to meetcha by the old highway."

Well, I realize that I've been hypnotized.

I love you Gypsy Eyes.

I love you Gypsy Eyes.

I love you Gypsy Eyes.

I love you Gypsy Eyes.

I been searchin' so long, my feet, they've made me lose the battle.

Down against the road, my weary knees, they got me.

Off to the side I fall, but I hear a sweet call;

My Gypsy Eyes is comin' and I been saved.

Oh 'n' I been saved.

That's why I love you.

Said I love you.

Love you

Lord I love you.

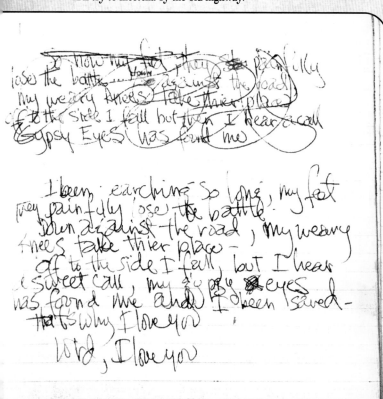

Jimi Hendrix THE LYRICS

Have you ever been, have you ever been to Electric Ladyland?

The magic carpet waits for you, so don't you be late.

Oh, I wanna show you the different emotions.

I wanna ride you with sounds and motions.

Electric woman waits for you and me.

So it's time we take a ride, we can cast all of your hangups over the seaside,

While we fly right over the loved filled sea.

Look up ahead, I see the love land, soon you'll understand.

Yeah, yeah.

Make love, make love, make love, make love.

I wanna show you

The angels will spread their wings, spread their wings.

I wanna show you

Good and evil lay side by side while electric love penetrates the sky.

I wanna show you

Lord, Lord, Lord I wanna show you.

Show you.

Yeah.

Have You Ever Been (To Electric Ladyland)

Hear My Train A Comin'

Well, I hear my train a' comin'.

Hear my train a', hear my train a' comin'.

I wait around the train station,

Waitin' for that train to take me away.

Lord, take me the hell out away from here.

Take me from this lonesome town.

Too bad you don't love me no more, baby,

Too bad your people put me down, put me down.

Tears burnin' me,

Tears burnin' me in my soul.

Whole lotta brothers getting'...

Tears burnin' me in my heart.

Tears burnin' me down in my soul.

Too bad you don't love me no more, baby,

Too bad your people, Lord, they made me go.

Hear my train a' comin'.

Hear my train a' comin'.

I hear freedom comin.'

I hear my train a' comin'.

I gotta leave this town.

Lord I gotta leave this town.

Gotta go on the road right now, baby.

Lord, I gotta be a voodoo chile, baby.

Go out in your world and become a magic boy, yeah.

Come back and buy this town,

Come back and buy this town,

An' give it all, give it all, give it all to you.

Yeah baby, make love to me one more time,

An', Lord, I gotta give, give it all to you.

All my love is for you baby.

You got proof to that.

Well, I hear my train a' comin'.

Hear my train a' comin'.

Hear my train a' comin'.

Hear my train a' comin'.

Hear my train a' comin'.

Lord, I hear my train a' comin'.

One of these days, I've got to be free.

Hear my train a' comin'.

Lord, I can hear my train a' comin'.

Hear my train a' comin'.

Hey baby, where do ya, ch, comin' from?
Oh, she looked at me and smiled and looked at this face.
And said, "I'm comin' from the land of a new rising sun."
Then I said, "Hey baby, where ya tryin' to go to?"
Then she says, "I'm gonna spread, spread around peace of mind,
And a whole lotta love to you 'n' you."

Girl, I'd like to come along.
Yes, I'd like to come along.
"Would you like to come along?" she asked me.
Yes, take a long ride now.

Hey baby, can I step into your world for awhile?
"Yes, you can," she said, "come on back with me for a ride."
We're gonna go across the Jupiter sands,
And see all your people one by one.
You gotta help your people out, right now.
That's what I'm doing here all about.

Yeah, yeah, may I come along?
May I come along?
May I come along?
Yeah, yeah.
Please take me.

Hey Baby (New Rising Sun)

His guitar slung across his back,

His dusty boots and Sears Cadillac.

A flamin' hair just a blowin' in the wind,

Ain't seen a bed in so long, it's a sin.

He left home when he was seventeen.

The rest of the world, he had longed to see.

And everybody who knows, boss.

A rolling stone gathers no moss!

Now you probably call him a tramp,

But it goes a little deeper than that!

He's a

Highway Chile!

Now, some people say he had a girl back home

Who messed around and did him very wrong.

They tell me it kind of hurt him bad,

Kinda made him feel pretty sad.

I couldn't say what went through his mind.

Anyway, he left the world behind.

And everybody knows the same old story;

In love or war you can lose little glory.

Now you probably call him a tramp,

But I know it goes a little deeper than that!

He's a

Highway Chile!

One more brother!

His old guitar slung around his back,

His dusty boots and Sears Cadillac.

Flamin' hair just a blowin' in the wind,

Ain't seen a bed in so long, it's a sin.

Now you may call him a tramp,

But I know it goes a little deeper than that!

He's a

Highway chile!

One more brother.

Don't let no one stop you.

Highway Chile!

Yeah yeah yeah

Highway chile

Rolling stone

Goin' down the highway

Rolling on

Highway Chile

Yeah yeah

Highway Chile

Rolling on

Ow!

Jimi Hendrix THE LYRICS

Look at the sky turn a hellfire red.

Somebody's house is burnin'

Down, down, down, down, down, down, down.

Well, I asked my friend, "Where is that black smoke comin' from?"

He just coughed and changed the subject and said, "Er, ah, I think it might snow some."

So I left him sippin' his tea

An' I jumped in my chariot and rode off to see just why and who could it be this time.

Sisters and brothers, daddy's mother standin' 'round cryin,

When I reached the scene the flames were makin' a ghostly whine.

So I stood on my horse's back an' I screamed without a crack.

I say, "Oh baby, why did you burn your brother's house down?"

Hey, Hey, Hey

Look at the sky turn a hellfire red, Lord.

Somebody's house is burnin'

Down, down, down, down.

Look at the sky turn a hellfire red, Lord.

Somebody's house is burnin'

Down, down, down, down, down.

Well, someone stepped from the crowd, he was nineteen miles high.

He shouts retired and disgusted, so we paint red through the sky.

I said, "The truth is straight ahead, so don't burn yourself instead.

Try to learn instead of burn, hear what I say."

So I finally rode away, but I'll never forget that day,

'Cause when I reached the valley I looked way down 'cross the way.

A giant boat from space landed with erie grace,

And came and taken all the dead away.

Hey, Hey, Hey

Look at the sky turn a hellfire red, Lord.

Somebody's house is burnin'

Down, down, down, down.

Look at the sky turn a hellfire red, Lord

Somebody's house is burnin'

Down, down, down, down.

Look at the sky turn a hellfire red, Lord.

THE LYRICS

F#

House burning down — Jim Hendrix

(chorus) look at the Sky Turn a hell fire red, he
Some body's house is burning —
down down down down — down down down

(1st verse) I ask my friend , wheres is that black
Smoke comeing from — he just coughed
and changed the subject, and
said "I think it might snow some" —

So I left him sipping his tea and
I jumped in my chariot and rode off to
see just why and who could it be This ti

2nd verse) Sisters and brothers, daddys, mothers
standing around crying ,
when I reached the scene , the DC flames
were makeing a ghostly whine , So
I stood on my horses back — and I
screamed with out a crack , I say
Oh Baby why did you burn your
brother's house down —

(repeat chorus) — then Guitar Solo —
3rd verse: Well Some one stepped from the crowd, he was 19
miles high; He shouts "Were Tired and disgusted
So we paint red through the sky "
I say the thruth is straight ahead — So don't
burn yourselves instead — Trying to learn instead of
burn" .. HEAR WHAT I SAY —
(over)

So I finally rode away but I'll
never forget that , cause when I
reached the valley, I looked way down
across the way
A Giant boat from space landed
with eerie grace and came and taken
All the dead away —

(Repeat chorus) —

I Don't Live Today

Will I live tomorrow?
Well, I just can't say.
Will I live tomorrow?
Well, I just can't say.
But I know for sure,
I don't live today.

No sun coming through my windows,
Feel like I'm livin' at the bottom of a grave.
No sun coming through my windows,
Feel like I'm livin' at the bottom of a grave.
I wish you'd hurry up 'n' execute me
So I can be on my mis'rable way.

Well, I don't live today,
Maybe tomorrow,
I just can't say,
But I don't live today,
It's such a shame to waste
Your time away like this.

Well, I don't live today.
Maybe tomorrow,
I just can't tell you baby,
But I don't live today.
It's such a shame to spend the time…
Away like this… existing…

Yeah!
Ow!
Yeah!
Oh no

There ain't no life nowhere.
Damn man… you experienced?
Get experienced
Get experienced!
Get experienced!
Are you experienced?

Yeah. Sing a song bro'.

If the sun refused to shine
I don't mind, I don't mind.
If the mountains fell in the sea,
Let it be, it ain't me.

Got my own world to live through and
And I ain't gonna copy you.

Now if a 6 turned out to be 9,
I don't mind, I don't mind.
If all the hippies cut off all their hair,
I don't care, I don't care.
Dig.

'Cause I've got my own world to live through and
And I ain't gonna copy you.

White collar conservative flashin' down the street
Pointin' their plastic finger at me.
They're hopin' that soon my kind will drop and die,
But I'm gonna wave my freak flag high, high!
Wave On, Wave On

Fall mountains. Just don't fall on me.
Go ahead business man, you can't dress like me.

Don't nobody know what I'm talking about?
I've got my own life to live.
I'm the one that's gonna have to die when it's time for me to die,
So let me live my life the way I want to.

There.
Sing on brother, play on drummer.

In From The Storm

Just came back ~~Baby~~
Just came back
from the Storm
— Repeat —

I didn't know then
but I was suffering
for my Love to keep
me warm.

Hey Baby thank you
for picking me up ——
It was cold down
Here crying rain was tearing me up.

the wind it woke me
up by suprise
~~the~~ crying Blue Rain
was burning my eyes
it is you - my love, who
~~brought~~ Brought me in
I love you much ; I'll
never ever stray from
you again

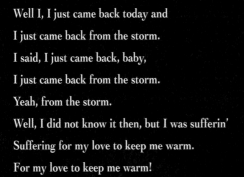

Well I, I just came back today and
I just came back from the storm.
I said, I just came back, baby,
I just came back from the storm.
Yeah, from the storm.
Well, I did not know it then, but I was sufferin'
Suffering for my love to keep me warm.
For my love to keep me warm!

It was so cold and lonely, yeah,
The wind and cryin' blue rain tearin' me up.
It was so cold and lonely,
Cryin' blue rain was tearin' me up!
Oh, tearin' me up!
I wanna thank you, my sweet darlin',
For diggin' in the mud and pickin' me up!
And that's so much!
Thank you baby!

It was a cryin' blue rain that's burnin' my eyes,
The wind and lightning struck by surprise.
It was you, my love, who brought me in.
I love you so much, I'll never stray from you again.

Hey!

I just came back today.
Just came back to get my baby on our way.
Yeah! Yeah!

It's too bad

Lord, my brother can't be here today

It's too bad

My brother can't be here today

But one time they came around to my house, you know

And I was kinda like out of my mind and sent him a crying away

I said, baby ya hear me cry

Baby, baby, hey baby hear, hear me cry

Remember that room full of mirrors I was telling you about

I said brotha, don't tell me you come around here to hustle like the rest of the people do

I said brotha, brotha don't tell me you came around here hustling like the rest of those

people do

And you say no, no brotha Jim, he said,

I just comin' here lookin' for life like you do

He say, don't forget I'm your brotha, baby.

I say that's what happens sometimes when you lose ya'self in a bend

And he looked at me, you know, he sees these two blondes laying around next to me

I say Lord, please don't lose yourself baby

That's what happens when you lose yourself on nothin'

He said, baby you know me, I'm your brotha please don't take me for nothin'

It's too bad, too bad

Lord, my brotha just can't be here with me today

It's too bad, my brotha can't be here with me today

But he came around my house, and ah, ask me to help him.

I say, man go to hell on your hustling ways

And I think they send him away to the war today

So I'll go way across the tracks, way across the tracks,

and man they treat me the same as you do too

Well I'll go way back over across the tracks and they treat me the same as you do

Say man until you come back, completely black, go back where you came from too.

Yeah

Yeah, yeah, yeah, yeah.

Izabella

Hey, Izabella,

Girl, I'm holdin' you in my dreams every night.

Yeah, but you know good love, baby,

Ya know we got this war to fight.

Well, I'm talkin' to you on the fire,

Well, I hope you're receivin' me alright.

Hey, Izabella,

Girl, I am fightin' this war for the children in you.

Yeah, yeah, yeah baby,

All of this blood is for the world of you, all your love.

So I hope you saved your love baby,

Then I know they'd find her true.

Hey!

Hey, Izabella,

Here comes the rays of the rising sun.

Here they come.

Well, I gotta go back out there and fight now, baby,

I can't quit until the devil's on the run,

On the run, yeah, yeah, baby.

So keep those dreams in confidence strong

Soon I'll be holding you instead of this machine gun.

Hey, Izabella,

Aw, sweet lover.

Spill all my blood for you.

Rock me baby.

Ahh! Hey, Izabella.

Jimi Hendrix THE LYRICS

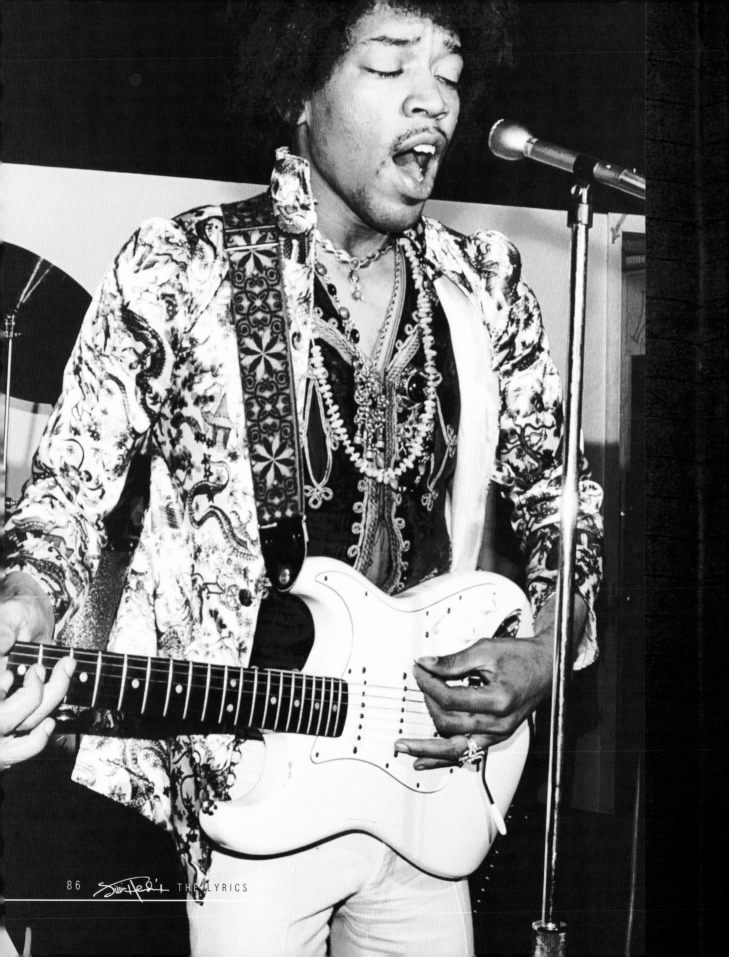

Little Miss Lover,

Where have you been in this world for so long?

Well, I love a lover,

That feels like you. Would ya like to tag along?

Well, I really don't need any help little girl,

But I think you can help me out anyway.

Aw, sock it to me.

Would you believe baby,

I've been lookin' for a soul that feels like you for some time?

Excuse me while I see

If the gypsy in me is right, if you don't mind.

Well, he signals me okay,

So I think it's safe to say I'm gonna make a play.

Ah, yeah.

Ya see me walk towards you baby.

Ah, yeah.

Talk you into a…

Ah, get into it.

Hey, hey, little Miss Lover,

Well, now there's so much you and me can discover.

But I think we should start,

Think we should start right now, baby.

Hey, hey little Miss, little Miss, little Miss, little Miss Lover.

Oh baby, look at me with soul here.

So good, little Miss Lover.

Hey baby.

She makes everything good.

Hey, lover, ah.

Little Wing

Well, she's walkin' through the clouds
With a circus mind that's running wild.
Butterflies and zebras and moonbeams and fairytales.
That's all she ever thinks about.
Riding with the wind.

When I'm sad she comes to me,
With a thousand smiles she gives to me free.
It's alright, she says, it's alright,
Take anything you want from me,
Anything, anything.

Fly on Little Wing.

Yeah, yeah, yeah, yeah little baby.

Jimi Hendrix THE LYRICS

"Long hot Summer Night   Jan. 17 1968

Long Long hot Summer night
as far as my eyes could see
But my heart was in a cold winter Storm
Oh my Darling, where can you be —

three sugar walls and two candy cane windows,
But Silvias mood melted all those in sight
Everyone's on fire — But I'm snowing in a blizzard
where are you on this hot cold repeat 2 times
where are you on this hot cold Summer night

BRIDGE
        Just then the telephone blew its horn across
the room — Scared little Annie clean out of her
mind . . . . . Roman the candle peeps out of
his peek-a-boo hide and seek and grabbed
little Annie from the ceiling just in time
And the telephone keeps on screaming
        Guitar Solo.

        over for the rest

Hello says my shakey voice on the phone,
well, How you doing
I start to stutter, can't you tell I'm done
fine —   It was my Baby talkin, She's O
way down cross the border

She says I'm gonna hurry to you, I been
a fool and I'm tired of crying

Long Long Hot Summer night
as far the eyes can see
I can feel the heat comeing on as my
Baby's getting closer
So Glad that my Baby's comeing
to rescue me   ect . . .

Hurry home on this Long Hot Summer
Repeat and fade out

Sure was,

It was a long, long, long hot summer night,

As far as my eyes could see.

Well, my heart was way down in a cold, cold winter storm.

Well, my darlin', where can you be?

Where can you be, baby?

Where can you be?

There were three sugar walls and two candy cane windows,

But the silliest mood melted all those in sight, all those in sight.

Ev'rybody's on fire but I'm a snowin' in a cold blizzard.

Where are you when there's a hot cold summer?

Where are you when there's a hot cold summer?

Where are you when there's a hot cold summer night?

Around about this time the telephone blew it's horn across the room.

Scared little Annie clean out of her mind. And I tell ya,

Roman Candle, he peeps out of his peekaboo hide and seek

And grabbed little Annie from the ceiling just in time.

And the telephone, it keeps on screamin', yeah, yeah, yeah.

"Hello," said my shaky voice, "Well, how you doin'?"

I start to stutter, "Look, can'tcha tell I'm doin' fine?"

It was my baby talkin', she's way down cross the border.

She says I'm gonna hurry to ya.

I've been a fool and I'm tired of cryin'.

Said, I'm tired Jimi.

Yes, a long, long hot summer night as far as my eyes could see.

But I can feel the heat comin' on as my baby's gettin' closer.

I'm so that glad my baby's comin' to rescue me.

Say, so glad that my baby's comin' to rescue me.

So glad my baby's comin' to rescue me.

They're comin' to rescue.

Woo!

Long, long hot summer night
as far as my eyes could see
But my heart was in a cold winter
storm - Oh my Darling, where can
you be ___
3 sugar walls and two candy cane
windows - But silvia's thoughts melted
all those in sight -
. Every body's of fire - But I'm snowing
in a blizzard .... where are you on
this hot cold repeat 2 times) where are you
on this hot cold summer night -

BRIDGE

Just then the telephone blew
it's horn across the room
Scared little Annie clean out of her mind
Roman the candle peers out of his
peek-a-boo hide and seek - And
grabbed little Annie from the ceiling
just in time
And the telephone keeps on
screaming ___ Guitar solo

Hello says my shaky voice
well, how you doing
~~yes~~ I start to ~~laugh~~, yes, ~~you~~ cant
you ~~to~~ tell im doing fine
It was my Baby, She's way on
down across the border

She says, I'm gonna hurry to you
I been a fool and ~~I'm~~ tired of cryin

Long long hot Summer night, as
far as the eyes can see

My Bed soak and wet ~~close to~~ for
hours since the call - Darling I'm
So glad you're come to me

Look over yonder, here comes the blues.

The thirteenth of anytime, qualified fools.

I can see 'em comin' wearin' a blue armored coat.

He's standin' there with your finest, hittin' wrong notes.

Look over yonder; he's comin' my way.

When he's around I never have a happy day.

And he even bust my guitar string.

Look over yonder.

Look over yonder.

Look over yonder.

Look over yonder.

Look over yonder.

Look over yonder.

Look over yonder.

Look over yonder.

Look over yonder.

Well, he's talkin' to my baby.

They found my peace pipe on her.

Now they're draggin' her away.

Lord knows we don't need

The devil like him beating us to the ground.

Well, he's knocking on my door.

Now my house is tumbling down.

Don't you come no closer.

The path is getting colder.

Get away from my door, baby,

Unless you wanna start another war.

Look over yonder.

Hey! Look over yonder.

Look over yonder.

Look over yonder.

Look over yonder.

Look over yonder.

 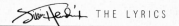

Is that the stars in the sky, or is it, rain fallin' down?

Will it burn me if I touch the sun, yeah, so big, so round?

Would I be truthful, yeah, in, uh, in choosin' you as the one for me?

Is this love, baby, or is it just confusion?

Oh, my mind is so messed up,

Goin' 'round 'n' 'round.

Must there be all these colors

Without names, without sound, baby?

My heart burns with feeling, but, uh

Whoah, but my mind, its cold and reeling.

Is this love, baby, or is it confusion?

Oh, my head is pounding, pounding,

Goin' 'round and 'round and 'round and 'round

Must there always be these colors

Without names, without sound?

My heart burns with feelin',

Oh, but my mind is cold and reelin'.

Is this love, baby or is it just confusion?

Oh, you tell me baby, is this love or confusion?

Mama, we must get together and find out...

Exactly what we're tryin' to do.

Love or confusion?

Confusion

Here he comes. I said, here comes your lover man.

Here he comes. Here comes your lover man.

Ah, I gotta get my head from this pillow

I gotta get outta here as fast as I can

Reach up, baby, hand me down my running shoes.

Reach up, baby, hand me down my running shoes.

I gotta get outta here, and I got no time to lose.

Here he comes, here comes your lover man.

Here he comes, here comes your lover man.

I gotta get my suitcase and get outta here as fast as I can

Here he comes

Here he comes, baby

Here he comes, baby

Here he comes, baby

(Here He Comes) Lover Man

Machine gun

Tearing my body all apart.

Machine gun, yeah,

Tearing my body all apart.

Evil man make me kill you.

Evil man make you kill me.

Evil man make me kill you,

Even though we're only families apart.

Well, I pick up my axe and fight like a farmer, you know what I mean?

And your bullets keep knocking me down.

Hey, I pick up my axe and fight like a farmer, now,

Yeah, but you still blast me down to the ground.

The same way you shoot me down baby,

You'll be going just the same, three times the pain.

And your own self to blame.

Hey! Machine gun!

I ain't afraid of your bullets no more, baby.

I ain't afraid no more.

After a while, your, your cheap talk won't even cause me pain,

So let your bullets fly like rain.

'Cause I know all the time you're wrong, baby,

And you'll be going just the same.

Machine Gun tearing my family apart.

Hey, yeah, alright.

Tearing my family apart.

Don't you shoot him down.

He's not to leave here.

Don't you shoot him down!

He's got to stay here.

He ain't going nowhere.

He's been shot down to the ground!

Oh, where he can't survive.

Yeah, that's one we don't want to hear anymore, right?

No bullets

At least here, huh.

No guns, no bombs.

Beverly Rodeo Hyatt House
360 North Rodeo Drive
Beverly Hills, California

Machine Gun.

1. Machine gun --- tearing my body
all apart.

Hey Machine gun ... tearing my
buddies all apart.

Evil men make me kill you

Evil men make you kill me

Evil men make me kill you

even though we're only families apart?

2. Well I pick up my ax and fight like
a farmer --- and your Bullets

Keep knocking me down — down to the ground

Hey I pick up my ax and fight like a natural

farmer now.. yea, But you still Blast me

down ... down to the ground —

the same way you shoot
Me down Babe, you'll going just the
Same.... 3 times the pain ... and
your own self to blame —

_____

3. I Aint ~~afraid~~ afraid of your ~~bullets~~ bullets Babe
aint afraid no more .
After awhile your cheap talk don't
even cause me pain ...
So let your Bullets fly like Rain .
Knowing all the time ^{THAT YOU WRONG} Babe ... ~~and that~~
you" be going just the same — 3 times the
drain, and your own self to blame —
Hey Machine gun ..

Manic depression is touching my soul.

I know what I want but I,

just don't know how to,

Go about getting it.

Feeling, sweet feeling,

Drops from my fingers, fingers.

Manic depression is a captured my soul.

Woman so willing, the sweet cause in vain.

You make love, you break love,

It's all the same when it's, when it's over.

Music, sweet music

I wish I could caress, caress, caress.

Manic depression is a frustrating mess. Wow!

Well, I think I'll go turn myself off and go on down.

All the way down.

Really ain't no use in me hanging around in

Your kind of scene.

Music, sweet music,

I wish I could caress, and a kiss, kiss.

Manic depression's a frustrating mess!

Ow! Ow!

Music, sweet music, sweet music.

Yeah!

Hmm, hmm, hmm.

Depression

Manic Depression

Waterfall, nothing can harm me at all,
My worries seem so very small with my waterfall.

I can see my rainbow calling me
Through the misty breeze of my waterfall.

Some people say day-dreaming's for all the
Lazy minded fools with nothin' else to do.
So let them laugh, laugh at me.
So just as long as I have you to see me through,
I have nothing to lose, 'long as I have you.

Waterfall, don't ever change your ways.
Fall with me for a million days, oh, my waterfall.

Well, I travel at a speed of a reborn man.

I got a lot of love to give from the mirrors of my hand.

I said, a message of love, don't you run away.

Look at your heart, baby, come on along with me today.

Well, I am what I am, thank God.

Some people just don't understand.

Well, help them God.

Find yourself first and then your tool.

Find yourself first, don't you be no fool.

Here comes a woman wrapped up in chain.

Messin' with that fool, baby, your life is pain.

If you wanna be free come on along with me.

Don't mess with the man, he'll never understand.

I said, find yourself first, and then your talent.

Work hard in your mind so you can come alive,

You better prove to the man you're as strong as him.

'Cause in the eyes of God you're both children to him.

Everybody come alive.

Everybody love alive.

Everybody love alive.

Everybody hear my message.

Beverly Rodeo Hyatt House
360 North Rodeo Drive
Beverly Hills, California

Message to Love

Ballad Content

~~told~~ We're traveling a speed
~~of a~~ ... of a reborn man
We got alot of love to give ...
from the mirrors of our hand —

— I said a message to love
don't you run away --- look at your heart Bib.
then come on ~~along~~ with me today —

Well I am what I am thank God
Some people just don't understand —
find yourself and then your too[First]
~~& I said~~ find your self first, don't
you be no fool —

Beverly Rodeo Hyatt House
360 North Rodeo Drive
Beverly Hills, California

Here comes a woman
wrapped up and chained
messing with those fools
keep your life's in pain

If you want to be free, come along
with me — Don't play with the man,
they never understand — —

I say find yourself first and then
your talent — — —
work hard in your mind, for it to come
alive. — And then show to the Man,
you're as strong as them...
Cause in the eyes of God,
we're all children to Him

Midnight Lightning

Midnight lightning flashin' all around me.
Lord, see it flashin' all around the trees?
See it flash our love all over me?

Wake up, my sweet darlin', and see the light upon your eyes.
Blue light flashin',
Shadows leap and church bells ring mad against the night.
Hey, my love, please stand up and watch me get down.

Midnight lightning flashin'
Flashin' all around our country house.
Thunder clashing.
See where the fields line all her trees in our little dream?

of a blues. Midnite lightning

I

Midnite lightning ——————
flashing ... all around my House ..-
Love ... please —— Hold me , Hold me -...
~~looks~~ ~~and~~ ~~strikes~~
                    crashing
tell me why ... it's ~~hitting~~ so close to 🌀
our trees and little scenes ——⚡——
                         they ring cheers.
2. Thunder ...clashing.. the church bells at 12 ⚡ .
                                              lightning
Blue light flashing ... Shadows leap in
~~flashes~~ ... ~ of nites —spent ... in the past
years of ⚡ the Barn full of —
full of witches and ghosts of dreams.
and ⚡ Happy Queens.

LONDONDERRY HOTEL

PARK LANE LONDON W1

Telephone 01-493 7292
Telex 263292
Cables Londhotel London W1

1. Midnite lightning.
flashing ... all around ~~the~~ the country house.
3. thunder ... clashing ————
~~So where~~ the fields light up on our
trees and our little dreams —
~~and all your schemes~~
2. A. Love ... come and see ~~How the sky~~
Or ~~could it be that your afraid to~~
B feel the light ~~upon your~~ eyes —

8. Blue light flashing ————
Shadows leap and church bells ring mad
~~against~~ the night.
Love ... please stand and watch with me
To night ——
feel the Soul of thunder crash ~~its~~ in the
fields ~~right~~ out side .. — — of our embrace —

P.2 (Bridge)

Sounds like — on the mountains
all the trucks are killing a highway.

feels like...
all the dams are breaking and surging our way.

it talks like ... 1,000,000 ocean's whispers

Taste like — the Blood ~~of~~ of the Sun
but ~~deeper~~ oh lord, much more deeper

Midnite, midnite Please don't
frighten my love away

Midnite - lightning
~~Striking~~
Tearing, through
the skies all around.
Wake up little Baby
Hear what the
Heaven's Shouting
about

So down and down and down and down and down and down we go.

Hurry my darling we mustn't be late for the show.

Neptune champion games to an aqua world is so very dear.

"Right this way," smiles a mermaid.

I can hear Atlantis full of cheer.

Atlantis full of cheer.

I could hear Atlantis full of cheer.

Lord, thank you.

So my Darling and I make love in the sand
to Salute the last moment ever on dry land —
Our machine, it has done its work, played its
part well without a scratch on our body and
we bit it farewell.
Star fish and Giant foams greet us with
a smile — Before our heads go under, we
take a last look at the killing noise of the
out of style

So Down and Down and Down and Down we go
Hurry my Darling, we mustn't be late for the
Show — Neptune champion games to an aqua
world is so dear. Right this way says a smiles a
mermaid, I can hear Atlantis cheer full of
cheer — — Down and down and down fade out

— 8b — My Friend —

D — Jan. 15 . 1968

I'm looking through Harlem, my ~~back door~~
~~and~~ stomach squeeled a little more) ← G⁷ A⁷ A
A stage coach full of feathers and foot prints
pulls up to my ~~door~~ soap box door —
A lady with a pearl handled neck tie, tied
to the drivers ~~neck~~ fence - breathed out bourbon
and coke possessed words (Guitar and vice harmony ᴮᴸᵁᴱˢ
(Haven't I seen you somewhere in hell or was
(it just an accident
Before I could ask was it the east or west
side, My feet, they howled in pain - the wheels
of her bandwagon ~~cut~~ very deep, But not as
deep in my mind as the rain
As they pulled away, I could see her words
stagger and fall on my muddy tent — I picked
them up, brushed them off to see what they said
("come round to my room with the teeth in the
(middle and bring along a bottle and a president
or ("come round to the room with the hole in the wall
And sometimes its not so easy - especially when your only
~~best I have~~ friend ~~that~~ sees, talks, looks and feels
like you and you see, talk, ~~look~~ ~~and~~ feel like him
do the same just like him

'well I'm rideing through - L.A
on a bycickle built for fools
I seen one of my old buddies, & he say
you don't look the way you used to do
I say, well some people look like a can box
He say look like you ain't got no coins to spare
I just picked up my pride from underneath
the pay phone and combed his breath right
out of my hair - Repeat verse

I just got out a scandinavian jail and I'm on my
way straight to you - But I feel so dizzy, I take
a quick look in the mirror to make sure my
friend's here with me too
And you think I don't drink coffee
So you fill my cup full of sand, But the frozen
tea leaves, at the bottom, cherry lipstick
around the broken edge. And my coat that
you let your dog lay by the fire on
And your cat, She attacks from her pill box
ledge. And I thought you were my friend too
My shadow comes in line before you
and fade out with "reflections" — reflections mirror mirror on the wall

Y'all pass me that bottle,

And I'll sing y'all a real song.

Yeah!

Let me get my key, ahem!

Well, I'm lookin' through Harlem,

My stomach squealed just a little more.

A stagecoach full of feathers and footprints

Pulls up to my soapbox door.

Now, a lady with a pearl handled necktie,

Tied to the driver's fence

Breathes in my face bourbon 'n' coke possessed words;

"Haven't I seen you somewhere in hell,

Or was it just an accident?"

You know how I felt behind all of that.

And so, before I could ask, "Was it the east or west side?"

My feet they howled in pain.

The wheels of a bandwagon cut very deep,

But not as deep in my mind as the rain.

And as they pulled away I could see her words

Stagger and fall on my muddy tent.

Well, I picked them up,

Brushed them off to see what they said,

And you wouldn't believe.

"Come around to my room with the tooth in the middle,

And bring along a bottle and a president."

And sometimes it's not so easy, baby,

'Specially when your only friend,

Talks, sees, looks and feels like you,

And you do just the same as him.

It gets very lonely out on this road, baby.

I got more to say…

Well, I'm riding through L.A.,

On a bicycle built for fools,

And I seen one o' my old buddies,

And he say, "You don't look the way you used to."

I say, "Well, some people look like a coin-box."

He say, "Look like, you ain't got no coins to spare."

And I lay back and I thought to myself,

And I said this,

"I just picked up my pride from underneath the payphone,

And combed his breath right out of my hair."

And sometimes it's not so easy,

'Specially when your only friend

Talks, sees, looks 'n' feels like you,

And you do just the same as him."

I just got out of a Scandinavian jail

And I'm on my way straight home to you.

But I feel so dizzy, I take a quick look in the mirror

To make sure my friends here with me, too.

And you know good 'n' well I don't drink coffee,

So you fill my cup full of sand,

But the frozen tea leaves on the bottom

Sharin' lipstick around the broken edge,

And my coat that you let your dog lay by the fire on,

And your cat he attacks me from his pillbox lair,

And I thought you were my friend, too,

Man, my shadow comes from mine before you.

I'm finding out that it's not so easy,

Especially when your only friend

Talks, looks, sees and feels like you,

And you do the same just like him.

Lord, he's so lonely.

Yeah.

Pass me that bottle over there.

1) She's just a nite bird
sailing thru the nite .
She's just a nite bird
making a midnite flight
~~From~~ she's flying
down to me — ~~But~~
~~says~~ But tommorrow I got
to set her free
So All we got - is one
precious nite — "ditto -
2) ~~by years~~ Throw your
Shoes and Blues
down down under the
bed —

She's just a night bird flying through the night.

Fly on.

She's just a night bird making a midnight, midnight flight.

Sail on, sail on.

Yeah, there.

Well, she's flying down to me,

But, 'til tomorrow, gotta set her free, set her free.

So, all we got, baby, is one precious night.

All we got is one precious night.

Put all your blues and shoes and things and rains down
under the bed.

Just wrap me up in your beautiful wings,

You better hear what I say, yeah.

Oh, carry me home.

But then take me through your dreams,

Inside your world I want to be.

Until tomorrow, no tears will be shed.

Hold on, 'til the sun gets out of bed.

Hold on, hold on, baby!

Fly on.

Sail on, sail on, sail on.

Sail on, carry me home, baby.

Just wrap me up
in your wings, hear
what I said carry me
Take me through your
dreams - Inside your
world, I want to be —
until tommorrow no
tears will you shed —
hold on till the
sun get out of bed

THE LYRICS

Lord, I had a woman,

Lord knows, she was good to me in ev'ry way.

Yes, I had a woman a real one.

Lord, she gave me lovin' all night and day.

I'm searchin', for my woman,

Or else, or else it's goin' to take me one million days;

Let me tell you something.

She way, way down in Dallas,

Way down in Texas land.

Lord, she had me wrapped around her wrist and one her finger.

Like a ring wrappin' 'round her third finger of a certain hand.

I'm lookin' for my Dallas honey bee.

Where can you be?

Where can you be?

Oh, help me.

Golden rose, the color of the dream I had

Not too long ago.

A misty blue and the lilac too,

A never to grow old.

Well there you were under the tree of song,

Sleeping so peacefully.

In your hand a flower played,

Awaiting there for me.

I have never laid eyes on you,

Like before this timeless day.

But you walked and ya once smiled my name,

And you stole my heart away.

Ah, stole my heart away, little girl, yeah.

Alright!

Golden rose, the color of the dream I had

Not too long ago.

Misty blue and lilac too,

A never to grow old.

Golden rose, the color of the dream I had

Misty blue and lilac too.

Golden rose, the color of the dream I had

Misty blue and lilac too.

Golden rose, golden rose, golden rose.

It's only a dream.

I'd love to tell somebody about this dream.

The sky was filled with a thousand stars,

While the sun kissed the mountains blue.

And eleven moons played across the rainbows

Above me and you.

Golden rose, the color of the velvet walls, surrounds us.

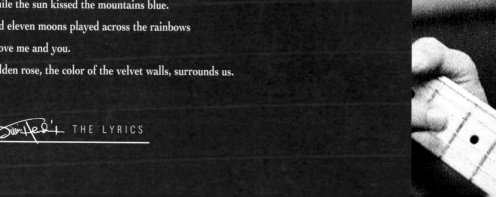

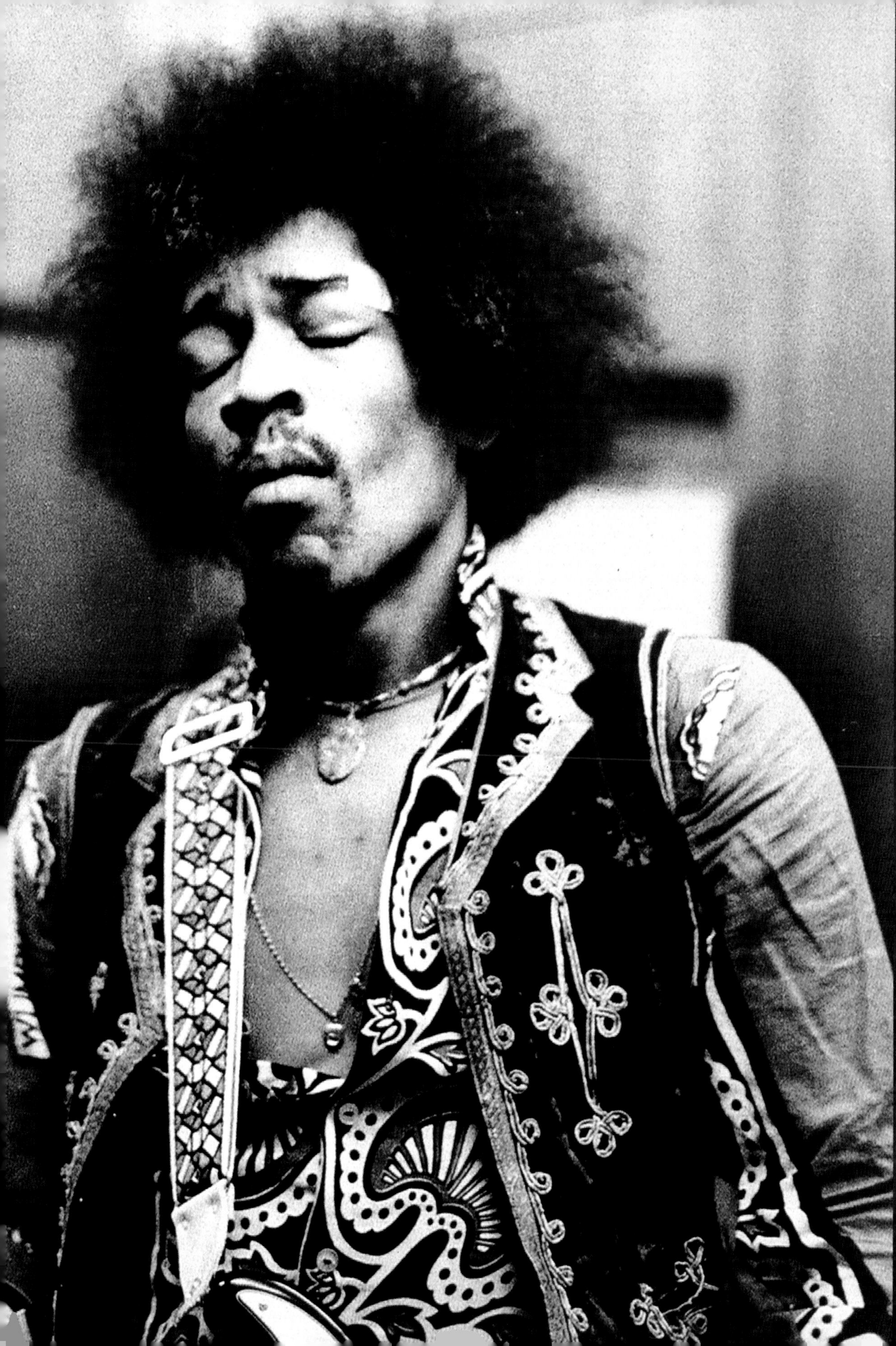

One Rainy Wish

Power of Soul

(1.) Shoot down Some of those airplanes
you been driving ~~no~~ especially
the ones that fly you too low —

Repeat.

Come on back up to Earth my friend
Come on back up with me
we all been ^through the Nite time Babe ᴮᵃᵇᵉ
Now let's reap the ~~waves~~ of reality —

With the Power of Soul
anything is possible
With the Power of you . Soul
anything you ~~need to~~ do — IS POSSIBLE

(2.) & Playing too much with one toy tends
to lead an escape into the foggy

ITS SO GROOVY TO FLOAT AROUND SOMETIMES

floatation is such a groove

Some times ... even a jellyfish

will agree to that —

Yea But old jelly's been floatin'
So long and so stack ... He don't
even have a bone in his jelly back

— Floating every day and every nite
riding high ... is a risk ... Sometimes

the wind aint right —

With the power of Sal
Any thing is possible —
With the power ... of you —
Any thing you got to do

Power Of Soul

Shoot down some of those airplanes you been drivin',
Especially the ones that are flying too low.
Shoot down some of those airplanes,
Especially the ones that are flying too low.
Come on back down to earth my friend,
Come on back up with me.
We all been through the night time, baby,
Darlin', sweet caress of reality.

With the power of soul
Anything is possible.
Anything is possible.

Flying so much with one toy, babe,
It's an escape to a far away land.
It's so groovy to float around sometimes,
Even a jellyfish will tell you that.
I said flotation is groovy and easy.
Even a jellyfish will agree to that.

Yeah, but that old jellyfish been floatin' so long and so
slack,
Lord, he ain't done got a bone in his jelly back.
Floatin' everyday and every night
Ridin' high, even if there's a risk.
Sometimes the wind ain't right.

With the power of soul
Anything is possible,
With the power of soul
Anything is possible,
With the power of soul
Anything is possible,
With the power of soul
Anything is possible,

with the power of you.
Anything you wanna do.
with the power of you.
Anything you wanna do.
With the power of soul
Anything is possible
Anything you wanna do.

Purple haze all in my brain.

Lately things they don't seem the same.

Actin' funny, but I don't know why.

'Scuse me while I kiss the sky.

Purple haze all around.

Don't know if I'm coming up or down.

Am I happy or in misery?

What ever it is, that girl put a spell on me.

Help me!

Help me!

Oh, no, no!

Purple haze all in my eyes.

Don't know if it's day or night.

You've got me blowing, blowing my mind.

Is it tomorrow, or just the end of time?

Ooh. Help me.

Ahh, yeah. Purple haze

Oh, no, no.

Oh, help me.

Tell me, baby, tell me!

I can't go on like this.

You're makin' me blow my mind.

Mama.

No, its painful, baby…

Purple haze.

Purple Haze
— Jesus Saves

Purple Haze...Beyond insane
Is it pleasure or is it
Pain —
Down On the ~~ceiling ceiling~~ ceiling
lookeing up ~~at~~ at the
bed... See my Body painted
Blue and red —

I see fetus unborns
~~Why is everybody~~
pointing at the Time ---
Rush through Space...
My Hair is Blowing in thier minds
~~paragdigs~~ through the Haze
I see 1,000 crosses
Scratched in the

Jimi Hendrix

Rainy Day, dream away

find out key

Rainy day, dream away,
let the sun take a holiday
flowers bathe and, see the children pla~

lay back and ~~groove~~ groove on a rainy d~

well I can see a bunch of wet preachers
look at 'em on the run
the carnival traffic noise, it ~~melts~~
sinks to a splashy hum —

Even the ducks ~~can~~ can ~~groove~~ groove
rain bathing in the parkside pool —
and I'm ~~just sitting here~~ leaning on my window
sill, digging ~~every thing~~ (EVERYTHING) and uh you too

Rainy Day, ~~dream away~~ Rain all day
aint no use in gettin uptight, just let it
groove it's own way —
        let it drain your worries away
lay back and groove on a rainy day —
lay back and dream on a rainy day

Rainy Day Dream Away

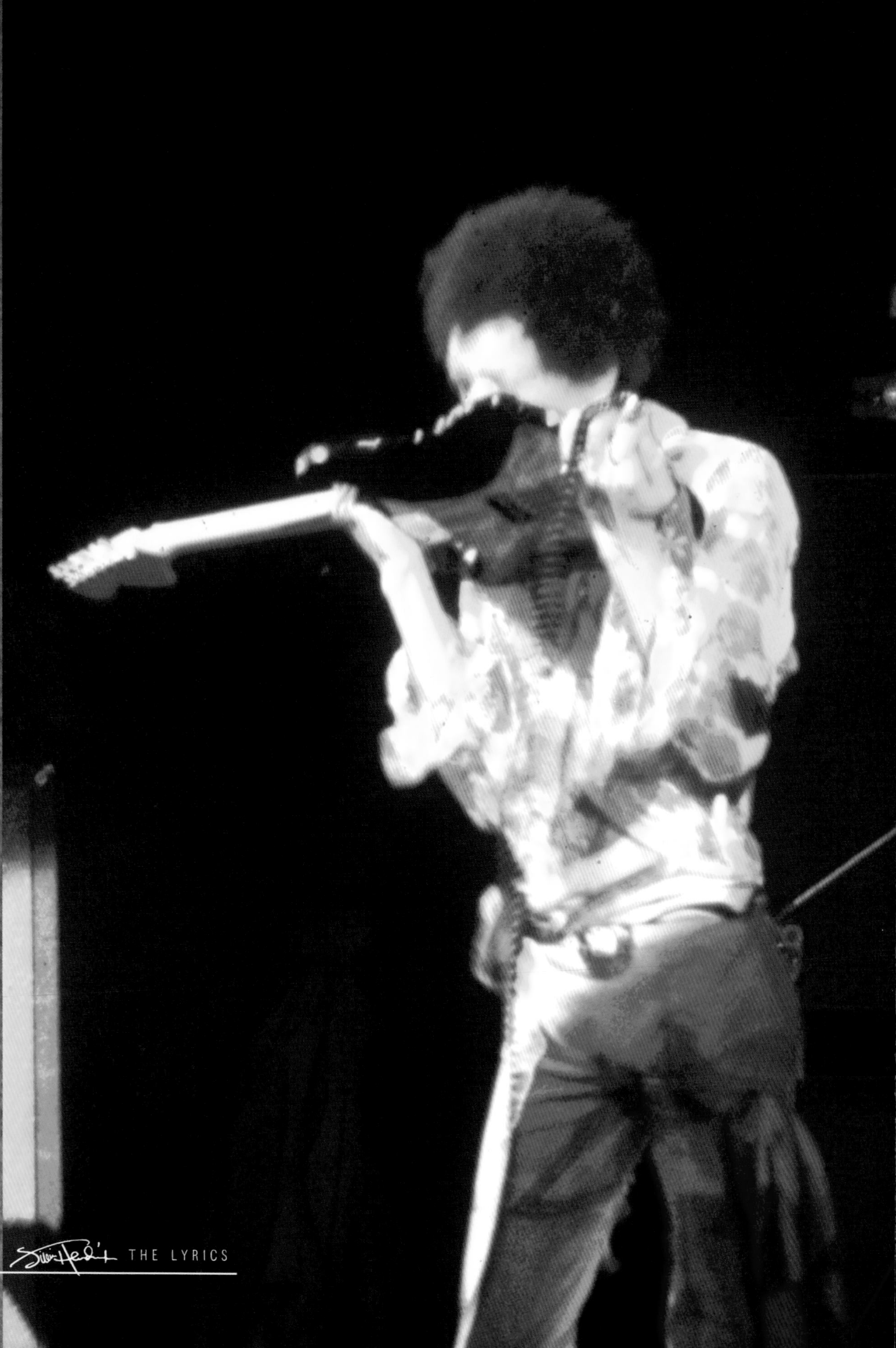

Hey man,

Take a look out the window 'n' see what's hap'nin'.

Hey man, it's rainin'.

It's rainin' outside man.

Ah, don't worry 'bout that.

Ev'rything's gonna be ev'rything.

We'll get into somethin' real nice, y'know?

Sit back and groove on a rainy day.

Yeah, ffft, mm,

Yeah, I see what you mean, brother.

Lay back an' groove.

Rainy day, dream away,

Ah, let the sun take a holiday.

Flowers bathe an' see the children play,

Lay back and groove on a rainy day.

Well, I can see a bunch of wet creatures,

Look at 'em on the run.

The carnival traffic noise, it sings, the tears splashing,

'N' even the ducks can groove.

Rain bathin' in the park side pool

And I'm leanin' out my window sill, 'n' diggin' ev'rything,

An' you too.

Rainy day, ah, rain all day.

Ain't no use in gettin' uptight,

Just let it groove it's own way.

Let it drain your worries away, yeah.

Lay back and groove on a rainy day.

Hey. Lay back and dream on a rainy day.

There's a red house over yonder,

That's where my baby stays.

Lord, there's a red house over yonder,

Lord, that's where my baby stays.

I ain't been home to see my baby

In ninety-nine and one half days.

Wait a minute, something's wrong here,

The key won't unlock this door.

Wait a minute, something's wrong,

Lord, have mercy, this key won't unlock this door.

Something's goin' wrong here.

I have a bad, bad feeling

That my baby don't live here no more.

That's alright, I still got my guitar. Look out now!

Yeah! That's alright!

Well, I might as well go back over yonder,

Way back among the hills.

Yeah, that's what I'm gonna do.

Lord, I might as well go back over yonder,

Way back yonder across the hills.

'Cause my baby don't love me no more,

I know her sister will!

Yeah!

Oh, remember the mocking bird, my baby bun.

He used to sing for his supper, baby.

Yes, he used to sing for his dinner, babe.

He used to sing so sweet,

But a since my baby left me

He ain't sang a tune all day.

Oh, remember the bluebirds and the honeybees,

They used to sing for the sunshine.

Yes, they used to sing for the honey, baby.

They used to sing so sweet,

But a since my baby left me

They ain't sing a tune all day.

All day.

Hey, pretty baby,

Come on back to me,

Make everybody

Happy as can be, yeah!

So baby, if you'll please come home again,

You know I'll kiss you for my supper. Yeah.

You know I'll kiss you for my dinner, baby, now.

But if you don't come back, you know I'll have to

starve to death.

'Cause I ain't had a kiss all day, now.

Aw, babe.

Please remember.

Got to remember.

Yeah!

Got to remember our love!

Come on back in,

Come on back in my arms.

Make everything that better.

Baby, hurry up now.

Can you hear me calling you back again, now?

Come on, baby!

Stop jiving around!

Hurry home, hurry home.

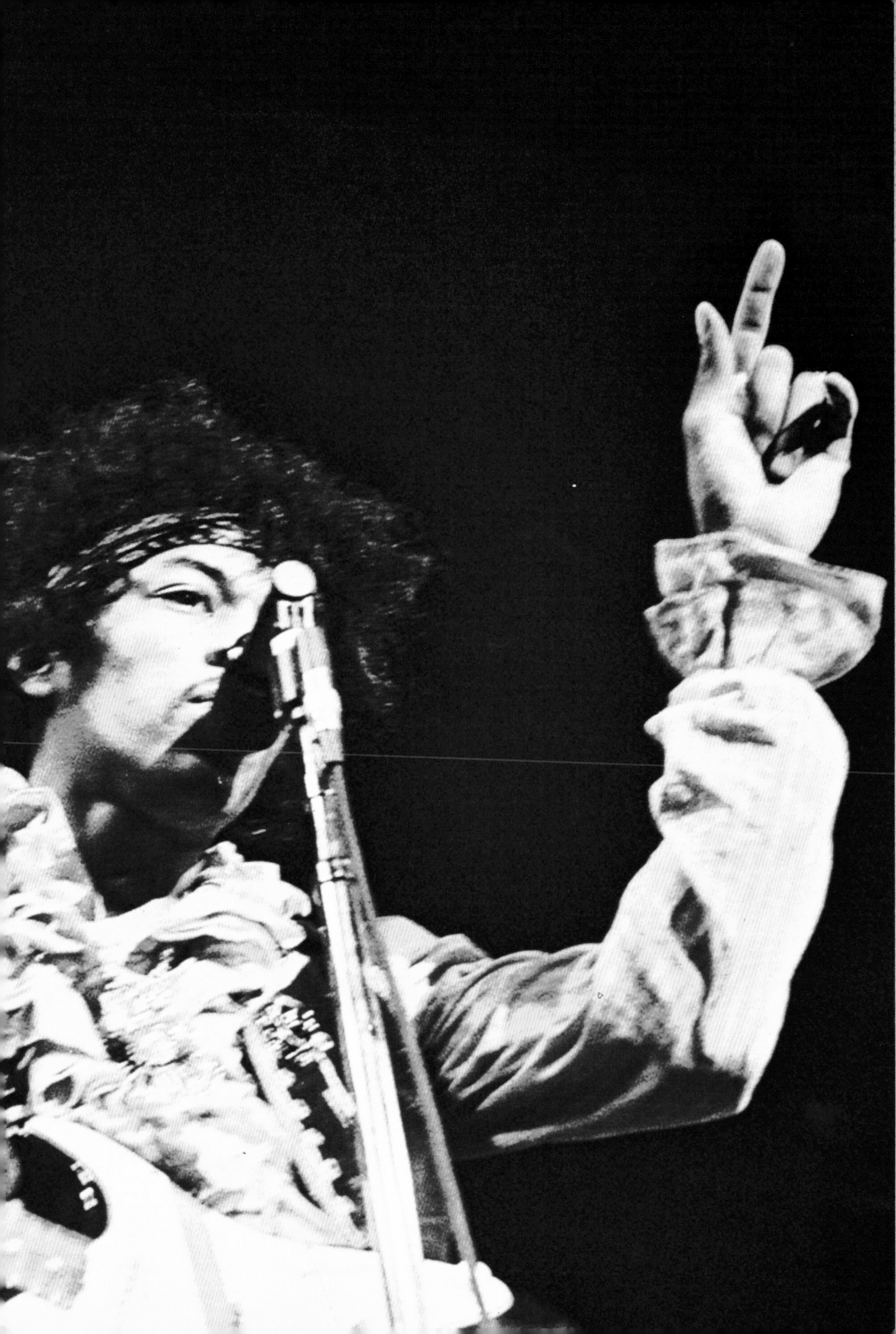

Remember

I used to live in a room full of mirrors,

All I could see was me.

Well, I take my spirit and I crash my mirrors.

Now the whole world is here for me to see.

...whole world is here for me to see.

...earching for my love to be.

...ght!

Yeah, yeah, yeah, yeah, yeah, yeah, yeah, yeah, yeah, yeah!

Dig this now.

Broken glass was all in my brain,

Cut and screamin', crying in my head, yeah.

Broken glass was all in my brain.

It used to fall out of my dreams and cut me in my bed.

It used to fall out of my dreams and cut me in my bed.

I said making love was strange in my bed, haha!

Yeah, yeah, yeah, yeah, yeah, yeah, yeah, yeah, yeah, yeah!

Oh yeah, yeah. Ohhhhh!

Yeah, yeah, yeah.

Yeah, yeah, yeah. Yeah, yeah, yeah.

No place (to) stumble. No place to fall.

Can't find the floor. No where at all.

See nothin' but sunshine all around.

Hang on Monday.

Love comes shine over the mountains,

Love comes shine over the sea.

Love will shine on my baby,

Then I'll know exactly who's for me.

Lord, I'd know who'd be for me.

In the meantime, which is a groovy time is to be.

I use to live ~~though~~ in a room
full of mirrors — All I seen
was me — Repeat
Well I ~~take~~ can't stand it
no more — So I smash the mirror
and set me free —
~~Broken I use to live in a room~~
~~full of mirrors~~

Broken glass all on the floor
Broken Glass in my head — Repeat
Broken Glass ~~come~~ ~~fell~~ through my
~~head~~ dreams fall and cut me
in my bed —

I find a ~~sex~~ sweet little girl
But she say "goodbye you
don't need me" Repeat
So I go to Detroit to find
an angel and she gives ~~me~~
~~Living of free for~~ ~~me her wings~~ ~~and sets I free~~ me her wings
and sets me free.
I use to live in a room of
mirrors : And I just might

I see fingers, hands, and shapes of faces

Reaching up and not quite touching the promised land

I hear pleas and prayers and desperate whispers singing

Oh Lord please give us a helping hand

Yeah, Yeah

Way down in the background

I can see frustrated souls and cities burning

And all across the water baby I see weapons barking out of the sand there

And up in the clouds I can imagine UFOs chuckling to themselves laughing they saying,

"Those people so uptight they sure know how to make a mess." Yeah!

Back at the saloon my tears mix and mingle with my drink

I can't really tell my feet from the sawdust on the floor

As far as I know they may even try to wrap me in cellophane and sell me

Brother sell me and don't worry about looking at the store

Yeah, yeah, yeah.

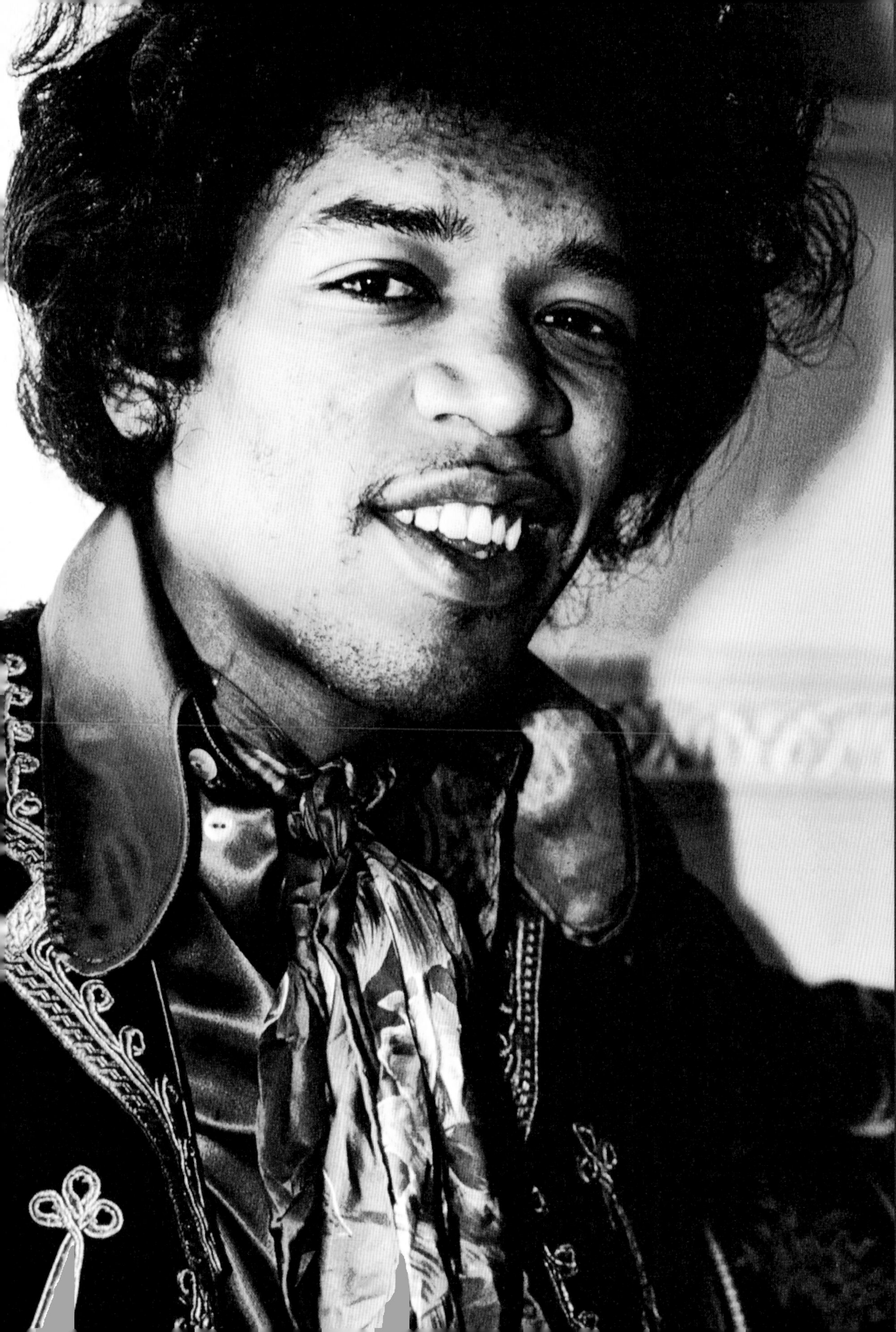

Somewhere

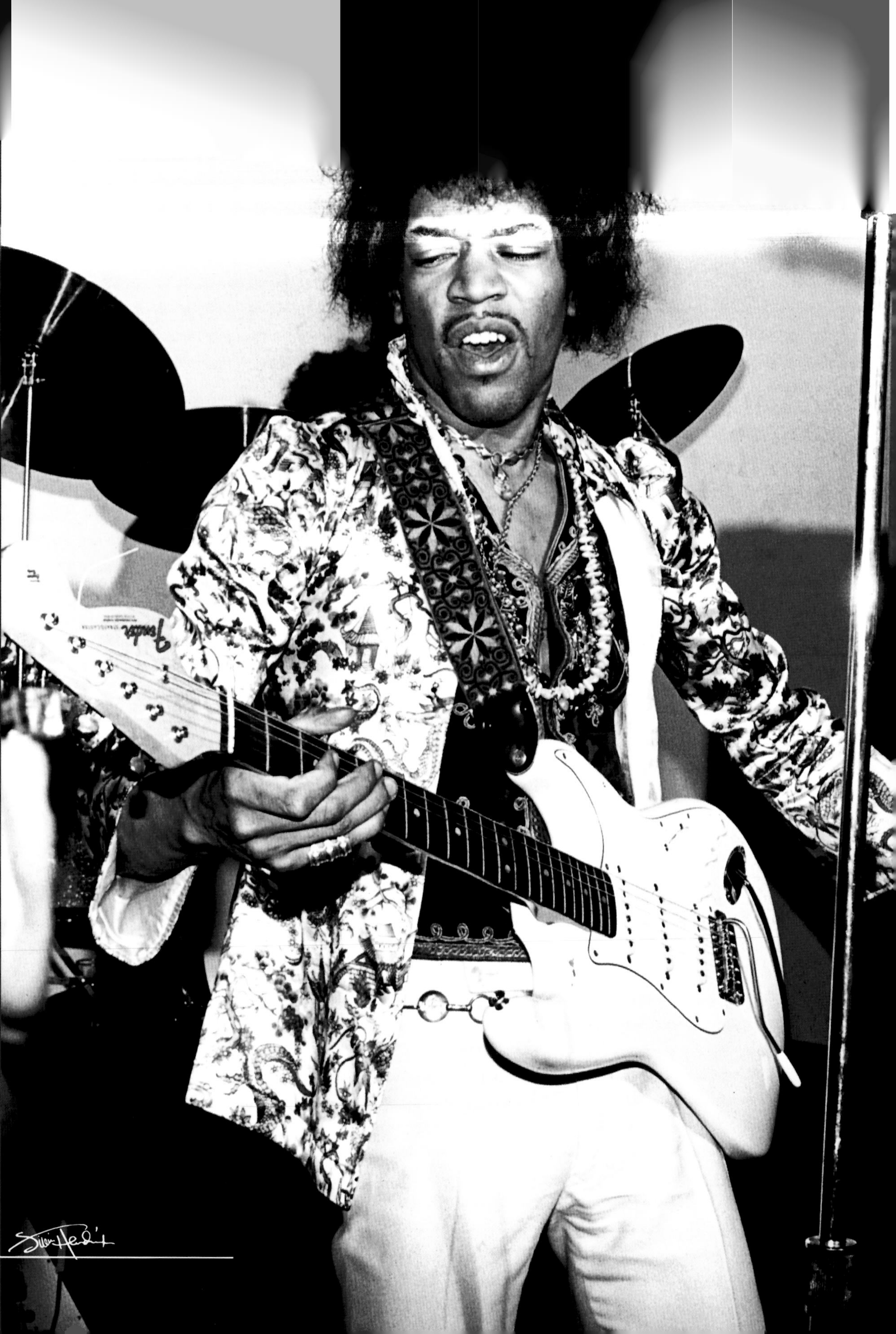

It's very far away.

It takes about half a day to get there

If we travel by my dragonfly.

No, it's not in Spain,

But all the same, you know it's a,

A groovy name,

And the wind's just right.

Hey!

Hang on my darling.

Hang on if you want to go.

Hear it's a really groovy place, it's a

Just a little bit of,

Said Spanish castle magic.

Yeah.

The clouds are really low,

And they overflow with cotton candy,

And battle grounds, red and brown.

But it's all in your mind,

Don't think your time on bad things,

Just float your little mind around.

Look out!

Hang on my darling.

Hang on if you want to go.

Really let me groove you, baby, with

Just a little bit of

Spanish castle magic.

Yeah, baby, here's some.

Yeah, ok babe, ok.

It's still all in your mind, babe.

Hang on my darling.

Hey, hang on if you want to go.

Oh girl!

That's right, babe, listen!

A little bit of

Spanish castle magic.

Hey, little bit of

Spanish castle magic.

Hey!

I can't sing this song, no.

Yeah, ok baby.

Get on baby!

It's all in your mind, baby!

Little bit of daydream here and there.

Yeah, everything's gonna be alright!

1. Well I'm a man ... at least I'm
trying to be —
   But I'm lakeing for ... the other
half of me ...
   Hey I'm a man ... Lookeing for my
      Love - to - be ...

   But ~~it~~ I aint gonna search ...
for Nothing   Desperatly —

   Till ~~then~~ ~~it~~ I'm feeling feeling fine
And I aint gonna cry ... ~~all the time~~ ...

2. Well you're a woman ... at least
you say you are —
   ~~then~~ I find you out ... In bed
with my guitar ...

   And you leave the real ... ME
outside ...
         Dont even care ... if I have
a ~~bokesooie~~ Heart inside —

   ~~it's easy~~ And in your hand ...
         a free ticket to ride

I'm a man ... at least
I'm ~~trying~~ to be —
   But I'm lookin for ...
the other half of me

   I'm looking for ...
that true love to be me

   But I aint gonna
search —
      for nothing desperately

   And I'm tryin so hard
Trying to keep my fool
   well I'm — trying so hard
Not to be a fool —

Ooh, way!

I sure got the blues this morning, baby!

Yeah, and I'm here to tell you about it...

So you might as well pick up on it.

I'm a man, at least I'm tryin' to be,

But I lived before the other half of me.

I'm lookin' for that true love to be,

But I ain't gonna search for nothin' desperately.

And I'm tryin', tryin' not to be a fool.

Well, I'm tryin', tryin', Lord, to keep my cool, baby!

Try so hard to keep it together.

After I find, baby, that true love of mine,

I'm just rollin', screamin', cryin'.

Flying can't be trusted, got busted.

Rolling stone, yeah.

You're a woman, at least you say you are.

You're a woman, at least you look like you are.

You're a woman, at least you taste like you are,

But you makin' off in bed with my guitar!

And then you leave off reel me outside.

You cry, cry to the moon and the nighttime.

You save my soul, you can't find,

But all you want is a ticket to ride.

After you showed me everything you prove otherwise,

You just rollin' screamin', cryin'!

Good lovin' sometimes, well, can't be trusted.

Stepping stone.

Stepping stone.

Stepping Stone

Still raining, Still dreaming   Hendrix

Rainy day, Rain all day
aint no use in getting uptight, just let it groove
    it's own way
let it drain your worries away
lay back and groove on a rainy day
lay dream on a rainy day

Rainy day, ah, rain all day.

Ain't no use in gettin' uptight,

Just let it groove it's own way.

Let it drain your worries away, yeah.

Lay back and groove on a rainy day.

Lay back and dream on a rainy day.

Lay back and groove on a rainy day.

Lay back and groove.

Hell yeah!

Lay back and groove on a rainy day.

Lay back and groove on a rainy day.

Lay back and groove on a rainy day.

Lay back and groove on a rainy day.

Lay back and dream on a rainy day.

Lay back and, lay back and, lay back, lay back and groove.

Lay back and groove on a rainy day.

Lay back and groove on a rainy day.

Lay back and groove on a rainy day.

Lay back and groove on a rainy day.

Lay back and dream on a rainy day.

Everyday in the week I'm in a different city.

If I stay too long the people try to pull me down.

They talk about me like a dog, talkin' about the clothes I wear.

They don't realize they're the ones who's square.

Hey!

That's why, you can't hold me down.

I don't wanna be down!

I gotta move on!

Stone free, to do what I please.

Stone free, to ride the breeze.

Stone free, I can't stay.

I got to, got to, got to get away right now.

Yeah! Alright!

Listen to this, baby.

Woman here, woman there,

tryin' to keep me in a plastic cage.

But they don't realize it's so easy to break.

Oh, but sometimes I get hot!

I could feel my heart kinda running hot.

That's when I've got to move,

before I get caught.

That's why, listen to me, baby,

You can't hold me down.

I don't want to be tied down.

I gotta be free!

Ow!

I said, stone free, to do what I please!

Stone free, to ride the breeze!

Stone free, I can't stay!

Got to, got to, got to get away!

Yeah!

Turn me loose, baby!

Yeah!

Stone free, to ride the breeze.

Stone free, to do what I please!

Stone free, I can't stay!

Stone free

I got to, got to, got to get away!

I'm Stone free right now!

Don't try to hold me back!

Ow!

Stone free, I'm goin' on down the highway!

Yeah!

Got, got, got, gotta, ah!

Stone Free

Bye, bye, baby!

Straight Ahead

Hello, my friend
So happy to see you again.
I was so alone,
All by myself, I just couldn't make it.

Have you heard, baby,
What the wind's blowin' 'round?
Have you heard, baby?
Whole lotta people's comin' right on down.
Communication, yeah,
Is comin' on strong. Oohh,
I don't give a damn, baby,
If your hair is short or long.
I said, "Get outta your grave."
Oh, everybody is dancing in the street.
Hey! Do what ya know, don't be slow.
You gotta practice what they preach,
'Cause it's time for you 'n' me
Come to fake reality.
Forget about the past, baby.
Things ain't what they used to be.
Keep on straight ahead.
Keep on straight ahead.

Straight ahead, baby.
Straight ahead, baby.

We gotta stand side by side.
They got to stand together and organize.
Said, "Power to the people," that's what they're spielin',
"Freedom of the soul."
Pass it on. Pass it on to the young and old.
You gotta tell the children truth, yeah,
They don't need a whole lotta lies.
Because one o' these days baby,
They'll be running things,
So when ya give 'em love, ya better give it right.
Woman and child, man and wife,
The best love to have is love of life.
Pass it on, baby.

Push it on, baby.
Straight ahead, baby.

Hello, my friend
It's so good to see you again.
Hey now, I been all by myself.
I don't think I can make it alone.
Lord, then if people keep pushin' ahead, oh no.
Lord, I think I've stayed too long.
You gotta keep pushing ahead, baby.

1. Have you heard — what the
wind's blowing round.
Have you heard — the all
the people is coming right on
down —
Communication ... is coming on
strong —

It don't give a damn ... if your
hair is short or long —
get out of your grave.
Everybody is dancing in the
street —
Do what you know (and don't be slow)
practice what you preach

'Cause it's time for you and
me   Come to face reality.
forget about the past Babe ...
things aint what they use
to be ——— (Keep it straight ahead) break-
we got to stand up, side byside;
... got to stand together and
organise ———
power to the people, freedom
for of the soul ———
pass it on to the young and old.

"You got to tell the children the truth ... ~~so~~ they don't need a whole lot of lies ...

~~You get tellig yourself~~

Because one of ~~these~~ these times they'll be running things

~~So when you give them love better~~

~~lot give love~~

@@ So when you give them Love ... You ^{better} make it right -

~~man~~ woman and child, man and wife the Best love to @ Have is the love of Life ___

Jimi Hendrix THE LYRICS

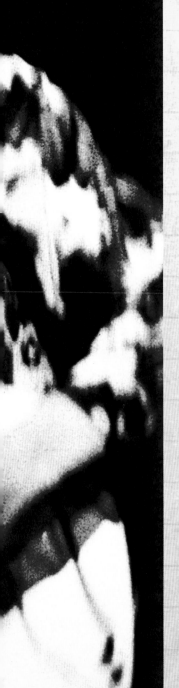

(Get out you bum, we don't want your kind in here anymore)

Layin' in the alley way,

Maybe some rich fool will come my way,

And throw me a dime,

That's all I need to get me more wine.

All I got is, to my name

Beat up guitar with three broken strings.

And I sure know

I just ain't taking care of no business.

Hey, Kitty Cat, where you goin'?

This part of the alley is my home,

Walkin' all over this side of my wall,

Boy, you sure gotta hold of that dog.

I had a sandwich in a paper bag,

But a rat stole it, ain't that some drag.

Lord, I know, I know,

I sure ain't taking care of no business.

Now I tried to get me a job,

Feedin' chickens and washin' down hogs,

But that meant standin' up all the time,

And standin' up to me is just like dyin'.

I'm so lazy that I could cry,

But tears are just too lazy to fall off my eyes.

Lord, Lord, Lord, Lord, I'm so messed up,

Can't even take care of no business.

Play it one more time

Yeah!

Oh, Woe is me

I sure wish I had me a sandwich, anything.

I'm so broke I can't even pay attention.

I'm so poor I couldn't even give you the time.

The stars up above that play with laughing Sam's dice,
They make us feel that it wants the world for us.
The zodiac rise, dreams that come through the skies.
It will happen soon for you.

Alright now, everybody, stick together now... Away we go!
Thank you very much for coming. Thank you! Thank you very much!
And now, we'd like to bring to you our one and only friendly
neighborhood experience-maker! Yeah! Alright, now listen!
Yeah... Baby... Thank you very much! The Milky Way express is
loading, all aboard! I promise each and every one of you, you won't be
bored! Now these next lines will keep everybody honest and straight.
What I'm really singing about is my brand-new pair of butterfly
rollerskates! Oh! Yeah, oh... Thank you, thank you! And I watch
them rise! Yeah... Uh, I'd like to say that there'll be no throwing
cigarette butts out the window. No throwing cigarette butts out the
window, thank you. I hope all of you brang your toothbrush... Yeah!
Okay... Now, to the right, you will see Saturn. Uh, ha! Outta-site!
Really outta-site. And if you look to the left, you will see Mars.
Yeah, okay. Yeah, okay. I hope you brang your parachute with you.
Hey! Hey, lookout! Look out for that door! Don't open that door!
Don't open that door! Oh... Well, that's the way it goes...
And now we're coming through the, uh, Milky Way section...
Yeah... It's where you form plates and stuff like that, Milky Way,
yeah... Yeah, everything's alright and outta-site! Whoa! Oh, no, it's,
uh... hahahah... hahaha! If you look around, you will see a few minds
being blown... Ha ha! It's happening, it's happening, baby! Yeah!
I hope you're enjoying your ride... I am! All the way! Yeah...
It's like I said... Goodbye!

THE LYRICS

After all the jacks are in their boxes,

and the clowns have all gone to bed,

You can hear happiness

Staggering on down the street,

Footprints dressed in red.

And the wind whispers Mary.

A broom is drearily sweeping

Up the broken pieces of yesterday's life.

Somewhere a Queen is weeping,

Somewhere a King has no wife.

And the wind cries Mary.

The traffic lights, they turn blue tomorrow,

And shine their emptiness

Down on my bed.

The tiny island sags down stream

'Cause the life that lived is, is dead.

And the wind screams Mary.

Will the wind ever remember

The names it has blown in the past?

And with this crutch,

Its old age and its wisdom,

It whispers, "No, this will be the last."

And the wind cries Mary.

Star fleet to Scout ship. Please give your position. Over.

I'm in orbit around the third planet from the star called the Sun. Over.

You mean it's the Earth? Over.

Positive. It is known to have some form of intelligent species. Over.

I think we should take a look.

Strange, beautiful, grass of green,

With your majestic silver seas.

Your mysterious mountains I wish to see closer.

May I land my kinky machine?

Although your world wonders me with your majestic

And superior cackling hen.

Your people I do not understand,

So to you I shall put an end.

And you'll never hear surf music again.

That sounds like a lie to me

Come on man, let's go home

 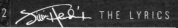

Try three little Bears

Ha Ha Ha says mama bear
as she irons daddy's holey under wear
Ha Ha Ha says daddy Bear as jim.
pours honey all on sisters hair

Ha Ha Ha say the little fish
as the fisher man goes home without a hitch
But Ha Ha Ha say the fisher man when
his lady burn french fries in the frying pan

And they all live happily ever after
Key change before Solo and in Solo three times

But He He He says You to me when you clip
my wings and then set me free.
and cry cry cry, oh I want to die cause
walking around on the ground instead of
up in the sky — and I just don't to live
for ever after —
what does this have to do with the 3 little Bears
well I was feeling blue Because I really care
(over)

that you're still gone from me
and I'm sad as I can be
So I'll sing and play this Tune
and try to laugh until you come back here
to me —
Togather we can live forever
after —

"Ha, ha, ha," says Mama Bear
As she irons Daddy's holey underwear.
And a "Hee, hee, hee," says Daddy Bear
As Junior pours some honey all on sister's hair.
And you know they all live happily ever after.

Well, "Ho, ho, ho," say the little fish
As the sad fisherman goes home without a hitch.
But aw "Hee, hee, hee," says the fisherman
With his lady bird french fries in the frying pan.
This is so silly, man.

"Hee, hee, hee," says you to me
(Man, I don't feel like going through with this, this is really silly)
Oh man, I want to die
'Cause walking 'round on the ground is really cramping my high.
I sure don't wanna live without you forever after, naw!

Now what does all this have to do with the Three Little Bears?
Well, I was just feeling blue, 'cause I really care
That you're still gone from me and I'm as sad as I can be
So I'll sing and play this tune until you come back home to me.

La La La, La La
La La La, La La…

BOUNCY BEAT

morris code type beat

It started from the SKIES
up

Hello... wait don't run away ~~I want to~~ *I won't touch* you .. don't runaway

I just want to talk
to you - I won't do you
No harm - I just want to
know about your diffrent
lives ~~or your~~ *this here* people form
I heard you have ~~brothers~~
your families liveing in
cages, tall and cold. and
some stay there *and dust* past the
age of old - is this true BREAK
please let me talk to you
DRUM + GUITAR BREAK

I just want to ~~a~~ know about
the rooms behind your minds
do I see a vacuum there
or am I going blind, or
is it ~~the~~ remains ~~of better love~~
of vibrations from echos long ago

age-old

~~listen for~~ things like love

the world ~~and so on~~ end

let your ~~fancy life~~ f low -

the way y ou want to

let me talk to you — DRUMS and guitar break

change tempo double slow

slow voices]   I have lived here

before the days of ice

of course this is why I'm so

concerned and I come

~~to~~ back to find the stars

misplaced and the smell

of a ~~something~~ that has burned

world

So where do I purchase

my ticket... I like to have

a ring side seat — I

want to about the new

mother earth - I want to

hear and see   EVERYTHING.

I just want to talk to you.

I won't do you no harm.

I just want to know about your

Different lives on this here people farm.

I heard some of you got your families

Living in cages tall and cold.

And some just stay there and dust away,

Past the age of old, is this true?

Please let me talk to you.

I just want to know about

The rooms behind your minds.

Do I see a vacuum there

Or am I going blind?

Or is it just the remains from vibrations

And echoes of long ago?

Things like "Love the world," and

A "Let your fancy flow."

Is this true?

Please let me talk to you.

Let me talk to you.

I have lived here before the days of ice.

And of course this is why I'm so concerned.

And I come back to find the stars misplaced.

And the smell of a world that's burned.

A smell of the world that has burned.

Yeah, well, maybe…

Maybe it's just a…

Change of climate.

Well, I can dig it.

I can't dig it, baby.

I just want to see.

So where do I purchase my ticket?

I'd just like to have a ringside seat.

I want to know about the new Mother Earth,

I want to hear and see everything.

I want to hear and see everything.

I want to hear and see everything.

Aw, shucks.

If my daddy could see me now.

Everything, everything, everything, ooh, everything.

Voodoo Child (Slight Return)

Well, I stand up next to a mountain
And I chop it down with the edge of my hand.
Yeah!
Well, I stand up next to a mountain
And chop it down with the edge of my hand.
Well, I pick up all the pieces and make an island,
Might even raise a little sand.
Yeah, 'cause I'm a voodoo child,
Lord knows I'm a voodoo child, baby.

I wanna say one more last thing.

I didn't mean to take up all your sweet time,
I'll give it right back to ya one of these days.
Ha!
I said, I didn't mean to take up all your sweet time,
I'll give it right back one of these days.
Yeah.
But if I don't meet you no more in this world, then
I'll meet you on the next one, and don't be late,
Don't be late.
'Cause I'm a voodoo child, voodoo child,
Lord knows I'm a voodoo child.
Hey, hey, hey!

I'm a voodoo child, baby.
I'll take me a look for an answer.
Question know.

Jimi Hendrix THE LYRICS

Voodoo Chile
Slight return

blue ... in California
And New York drowns as we hold hands
Voodoo Chile slight return
Well I stand up next to a mountain
and I chop it down with the edge of
my hand repeat
I take up all the pieces and make
an Island ... might even raise a little
Sand. Cause I'm a Voodoo Chile Voodoo Chile, lord knows I'm a Voodoo Chile
I didn't mean take up your sweet
Time. I'll give you one of these days repeat
If I don't see you no more in this world
I'll meet you on the next one
and don't be late, don't be late
cause a ...

---

key of E

Voodoo Child (slight return)   Jimi Hendrix

Well I stand up next to a mountain -
And I ... chop it down, with the edge of (my) hand
    Repeat.
Well I pick up all the pieces and make
an Island ... might even raise just
a little sand
        Cause I'm a Voodoo Child, Voodoo child
        Lord knows I'm a voodoo child, babe ...

I didn't mean to take up all your sweet Time,
    I give it to
            I'll give it right back to you,
(One of these days - (hah)
        I didn't mean to take up all your sweet Time -
    I'll give it right back one of these days

And if I don't meet you no more in this
world then I'll uh, I'll meet you on the next
on and don't be late, don't be late -
        Cause I'm a Voodoo Child, voodoo child
the lord knows I'm voodoo child

Voodoo Chile   Pt 1

Hp night I   [illegible]   2nd slightly return [illegible]

Moon Turned a fire red

My poor Mother cried, the Gypsie was
right, and she fell right down dead

Mountain lions found ~~me~~ me there waiting
2nd set me on an eagles wing

He took me ~~past~~ the outskirts of infinity
and when he brought me back
He gave me venus witche's ring
And he said fly on solo adlib, you're on
your own
And I'm a Voodoo Chile

well, I make love to you in your sleep
~~And you felt no pain~~ Lords know you
felt no pain
I could ~~I am~~ a million miles
and ~~to~~ right here ~~to~~ your picture frame
                          inside

Well, I'm a voodoo chile.
Lord, I'm a voodoo chile.

Well, the night I was born,
Lord, I swear the moon turned a fire red.
The night I was born,
I swear the moon turned a fire red.
Well, my poor mother cried out, "Lord, the gypsy was right,"
An' I see'd her fell down right dead.

Well, mountain lions found me there waiting
And set me on a eagle's back.
Well, moutain lions found me there,
And set me on a eagle's wing.
It's the eagle's wing, baby.
What'd I say?
Well, he took me past the outskirts of infinity,
And when he brought me back,
He gave me Venus witch's ring.
Hey! And he said, "Fly on, fly on."
'Cause I'm a voodoo chile, baby,
Voodoo chile.
Hey! Yeah!

Well, I'd make love to you
And Lord knows you'll feel no pain.
Yeah!
Say I make love to you in your sleep,
And Lord knows you felt no pain.
Have mercy.
'Cause I'm a million miles away,
And at the same time I'm right here in your picture frame.
Yeah! What'd I say now!
'Cause I'm a voodoo chile,
Lord knows I'm a voodoo chile.
Yeah!

Yeah, go 'head on boy.
Go 'head on little Stevie.

Well, my arrows are made of desire,
From far away as Jupiter's sulphur mines.
Say my arrows are made of desire,
From far away as Jupiter's sulphur mines.
Way down by the methane sea, heh, heh.
I have a hummin' bird that'll hum so loud,
You'd think you were losin' your mind.

Well, I float in liquid gardens
And Arizona new red sand.
Yeah!
I float in liquid gardens,
Way down in Arizona red sand.
Well, I'll taste the honey from a flower named blue,
Way down in California 'n' the New York drowns as we held
hands.
Yeah!
Hey, 'cause I'm a voodoo chile,
Lord knows, I'm a voodoo chile.
Yeah!

Well, I'm standing here freezing
Inside your golden garden,
Got my ladder
Leaned up against your wall.
Tonight's the night
We planned to run away together
Come on, Dolly Mae,
There's no time to stall.
But now you're telling me...

...Think we better wait 'til tomorrow.
Hey, yeah, hey.
Girl, what 'chu talkin' 'bout?
Yeah, yeah, yeah.
Got to make sure it's right,
So until tomorrow, goodnight.

Oh, what a drag.

Oh, Dolly Mae,
How can you hang me up this way?
Oo, on the phone you said
You wanted to run off with me today.
Now I'm standing here
Like some turned down serenading fool,
Hearing strange words stutter
From the mixed up mind of you.
And you keep tellin' me...

...Think we better wait 'til tomorrow.
What are you talkin' 'bout?
No, can't wait that long.
Oh, no.
Got to make sure it's right,
Until tomorrow, goodnight.

Let's see if I can talk to this girl a little bit here.

Dolly Mae, girl,
You must be insane,
So unsure of yourself
Leaning from your unsure window pane.
Do I see a silhouette
Of somebody pointing something from a tree?
Click, bang, what a hang,
Your daddy just shot poor me.
And I hear you say,
As I fade away...

Don't have to wait 'til tomorrow.
Hey!
Won't have to wait 'til tomorrow.
What you say?
Wait 'til tomorrow.
It must not have been right,
So forever, goodnight,
Listen at 'cha.
Ah! Do I have to wait?
Don't have to wait.
It is a drag on my part.
Don't have to wait
Don't have to wait
Don't have to wait
Don't have to wait
Don't have to wait
I won't be around tomorrow.
Don't have to wait.
Goodbye, bye, bye!
Oh, what a mix up.
Oh, you gotta be crazy.
Ow! Don't have to wait 'til tomorrow.

~~Hollywood~~

who knows?

1. They don't know like I know, do you know
   ~~what I know~~ I don't know -
   What my Baby's ~~been~~ putting down
   What my Baby's been putting down lately

2. Just came back from ... Mexicalli -
   Just came back in town - looking for my
   Sally - Have you Seen her ...Have you
   Seen Her ... Talking bout my ~~Baby~~ Baby
   Talking about my Baby -

3. Just came in ~~Just came~~ Just came
   in today - Just came in ...
   She's Spreading magic Honey -
   all in my Bed -

Beverly Rodeo Hyatt House
360 North Rodeo Drive
Beverly Hills, California

She got chains... attached to
my head -
Talkin about, talking about my bar
Well I don't know about her -
But she made me break a string
trying to get to her -
- They don't know...
W like I know -
She didn't know
like She didn't care
and I'm just hanging around
While she was walking
down the street with everybody
singing and humming, this tune.

Jim Hendrix THE LYRICS

They don't know

Like I know.

Do you know?

I don't know

What my baby

Puttin' down.

What my baby

Puttin' down, babe.

I just came back from

Mexicali.

Just came back in town.

Lookin' for my Sally.

Uh, have you seen her?

Oh, have you seen her?

Talkin' about my baby.

Talkin' about my baby.

Just came in.

Just came in, babe.

Just came in.

Just came in.

Spreadin' magic honey

All in my bed.

She got chains

Attached to my head.

Talkin' about,

Talkin' about,

Talkin' about my baby.

Uhh, I don't know about it.

They don't know

What I know.

They don't know

Like I know.

All the time, uh,

I been hangin' around.

All the time

I been hang(in') around.

She didn't know.

Ah, she didn't care.

She didn't know.

She didn't care, yeah.

And she go walking down the street saying "Yeah."

Everybody, da, da, da, da.

Do, do, do, do.

They don't know.

Nobody knows.

They don't know.

Just don't know.

Dah, do, do, dah, do, do, dah.

Well, you got me floatin' around and 'round.

Always up, you never let me down.

The amazing thing; you turn me on naturally,

Oh, and I kiss you when I please.

We're floatin' 'round and 'round.

Hey! Touch the ceiling, babe.

Got me floatin' naturally.

Yeah!

Now ya, ya got me floatin' across and through.

You make me float right on out to you.

There's only one thing I need to really get me there,

Is to hear you laugh without a care.

What I say now, ah.

Hey! Huh, 'round and 'round.

Got me floatin'.

Whoa, hey!

Got me floatin' nat'rally.

Floatin'.

Got me floatin'. Ooh.

Yeah!

Gimme one more time, brother, say it.

Got me floatin', yeah.

See the sky?

Look up.

Now, your daddy's cool and your momma's no fool.

They both know I'm heads over heels for you.

And when the day it melts down into a sleepy, red glow,

That's when my desires start to show.

Hey! Hey!

Got me floatin'.

Touch the sky.

You got me floatin'.

Hey, hey, hey,

Hey, now, hey-o.

Floatin' hey, hey!

Ow! Hey!

Got me floatin.'

SPECIAL THANKS

Jimi's God-inspired lyrical mastery came from his heart and soul leaving to us

a part of him that will forever live on through word & song.

His music continues to be the soundtrack of our lives and the words are an inspiration to our journey.

I want to first thank my father, Al Hendrix, for always encouraging us to be

unique, loyal and to give more than you take. God rest his soul.

My loves: Sheldon Reynolds, Austin, Quinntin, Claytin, & Langstin.

Also thanks go out to the following for your love, support & encouragement in completing

this beautiful labor of love: John McDermott, Bob Hendrix, Amanda Howell, Lin Anderson,

Steve Pesant, Kim Hanson, Experience Hendrix, Phil Yarnall, Stan Stanski, SMAY, Eddie Kramer,

Peter Kavanaugh, John Cerullo, Jim Fricke, EMP.

All songs written by Jimi Hendrix and published by Experience Hendrix, LLC (ASCAP)

PHOTOGRAPHY CREDITS:

Cover Photograph By: Chuck Boyd/Authentic Hendrix LLC

Back Cover Photograph By Eddie Kramer/Ariaphotos.com

Inside Jacket Photograph By: James A. Hendrix/Authentic Hendrix LLC

Book Photography By:

Chuck Boyd/Authentic Hendrix LLC (p. 10-11, 13, 14-15, 25, 30-31, 38-39, 40-41, 42-43, 44-45, 50-51, 52-53, 60-61, 62-63, 66-67, 68-69, 73, 78-79, 92-93, 96-97, 102-103, 104-105, 110, 120-121, 122-123, 128-129, 138-139, 148-149, 154-155, 160-161),

Torben Dragsby/Authentic Hendrix LLC (p. 2, 8-9, 54), Richard Chase/Authentic Hendrix LLC (p. 6, 12),

Ulrich Handl/Authentic Hendrix LLC (p. 20-21, 88-89, 162-163), Marshal Haglar/Authentic Hendrix LLC (p. 34-35, 58-59, 145),

Don Nix/Authentic Hendrix LLC (p. 70-71, 82-83, 86-87), Joe Cestaro/Authentic Hendrix LLC (p. 76-77, 156),

Wilson Lindsey/Authentic Hendrix LLC (p. 16-17, 48-49, 84, 142), Richard Peters/Authentic Hendrix LLC (p. 94-95),

James A. Hendrix/Authentic Hendrix LLC (p. 135), Andy Henderson/Authentic Hendrix LLC (p. 167),

Jan Blom/Authentic Hendrix LLC (p. 56-57, 98, 106-107, 126-127, 131, 132-133, 136-137),

Authentic Hendrix LLC (p. 36-37, 47, 76-77, 80-81, 114-115, 140-141, 146-147, 158-159)